THE DOG STAR

Will the Dog Star guide her father safely home?

With her father at sea on the packet *Jenet Rae*, Amy MacFarlane has to look after the family while working as a maid for the Paslew family. Amy is sure her sister Fanny is making a mistake in marrying Theodore Buxton, especially when she overhears Theodore and his brother Nicholas arguing about a mysterious money-making scheme. When it looks as though Theodore has involved her brother Rory in criminal activities Amy looks for help, but should it be from Dan Ainsworth, her childhood friend, or from Gilbert Paslew, her employers' son?

THE DOG STAR

The Dog Star

by

June Davies

Dales Large Print Books
Long Preston, North Yorkshire,
BD23 4ND, England.

British Library Cataloguing in Publication Data.

Davies, June
  The Dog Star.

  A catalogue record of this book is
  available from the British Library

  ISBN 978-1-84262-662-7 pbk

First published in Great Britain 2008
by D. C. Thomson & Co Ltd.

Copyright © June Davies 2008

Cover illustration © Andy Walker by arrangement with
P.W.A. International

The moral right of the author has been asserted

Published in Large Print 2009 by arrangement with
June Davies

Dales Large Print is an imprint of Library Magna Books Ltd.

Printed and bound in Great Britain by
T.J. (International) Ltd., Cornwall, PL28 8RW

Searching For Rory

Amy MacFarlane lay wide awake under the eaves of Clockmaker's Cottage, staring up at the low beams that crossed the ceiling of the bedroom she shared with her sisters.

Although exhausted after her long day's work as a maidservant at Whiteladies Grange, sleep would not come to her, her mind constantly replaying the bitter argument she'd overheard the previous evening between her elder sister's betrothed and his younger brother.

Restless, she turned on to her side to gaze out of the widow at the starlit sky, with Theodore and Nicholas Buxton's angry words still churning around her head.

It wouldn't be daylight for hours yet, and the tide was still far out, she knew, yet the sound of its soft rush whispered across the night air to creep in through the open window of the stone cottage overlooking the bay at Monks Quay.

Both of her sisters were sleeping soundly and, as she shifted her position to be more comfortable, Amy was careful not to disturb Fanny, who lay next to her, extract of eyebright soaking the muslin pads upon her closed eyes, and her shining fair hair coiled into curlrags. Fanny was determined to look her best for her wedding day.

Amy frowned, wishing she didn't have such feelings of foreboding about her sister's forthcoming marriage, but she'd never quite trusted Theodore Buxton.

He was just too good to be true. Too handsome. Too charming. Too perfect. And he came from a sophisticated background, far removed from the MacFarlanes' down-to-earth way of life at Monks Quay.

Should she have told Fanny – warned her – and related everything she'd overheard the previous evening, up at Whiteladies Grange?

It had been during the lull before dinner, and Amy had just finished tidying Gilbert Paslew's dressing-room, remembering to leave a new tablet of sandalwood soap next to his pitcher and basin, and had been about to slip through the adjoining door into the guest room to turn down the bed and to leave fresh towels, when she'd heard Theodore Buxton's voice, and had ducked back inside.

It was probably foolish, but she felt uncomfortable and tongue-tied whenever she bumped into either of her future brothers-in-law here at Whiteladies, where she was but a servant and they the guests of her master, Alfred Paslew, Gilbert's father.

The Buxton brothers were already deep in heated conversation as they approached along the passageway and, as they entered the guest room, Amy was taken aback at the agitation in Nicholas's normally quiet voice.

'It's no use, Theo!' he was saying. 'You shall not talk me round to your way this time! I can't imagine why I ever let you persuade me to go along with your plans in the first place!'

'Because, dear boy, you know this is the perfect scheme!' Theodore replied carelessly.

Amy peered through the slightly open door that connected with the adjoining room and saw that he'd paused to light a cigar.

'Besides, what options have we?' he went on. 'The first son inherits the family pile and the second goes into the army. Well the least said about the Buxton family pile the better, and you haven't the slightest aptitude for going to some far-flung corner of the Empire and subduing the natives! You just don't have the stomach for a fight, Nick!'

'I don't have the stomach for this – this – deception!'

'May I remind you who it was who brought me to Whiteladies last summer to visit your old school chum?' snapped Theodore. 'You made the introductions and I simply made the best use of them! Is it my fault old Paslew's greed knows no bounds? He almost bit my hand off when I mentioned those shares!'

'Yes, but–'

'But nothing!' cut in Theodore, pouring himself a whisky. 'You knew my motives for coming to Whiteladies, although even I could not have anticipated the astounding success of the venture! Paslew is like all men of his sort – however much money and power they acquire, it's never quite enough!'

'It's not Alfred Paslew and his wretched money I'm worried about. He's a businessman. And pretty ruthless too, by all accounts,' pressed on Nicholas. 'It's Fanny, and the MacFarlanes, that I'm concerned about.'

'What about them?'

'It's gone far enough, Theo!' responded Nicholas fervently, and from the gap in the doorway, Amy could see how pale and upset he looked. 'You should tell Fanny the truth.'

Theodore's handsome face looked suddenly sly. 'Taken a shine to the girl yourself,

10

have you? Can't say I'm surprised. Fanny does have the face of an angel! And such dainty, vain manners despite hailing from a cultural desert like Monks Quay. She's a spirited filly, too. I couldn't have chosen better.'

'Then be honest with her!' demanded Nicholas. 'For goodness' sake, Theo, you're getting married in a couple of days and Fanny has all those false impressions you've given her!'

'Calm down! What have I done to Fanny or her family that is so dreadful? I proposed to the girl!' he exclaimed, sitting in one of the winged chairs at the side of the fireplace. 'Fanny MacFarlane wants a husband and to escape from this godforsaken speck on the map, and I need an attractive wife who looks and behaves like a lady yet whose family are simple folk who don't ask too many questions. We both of us are getting what we want. What's so wrong with that? Fanny loves me and I absolutely adore her. You're not about to spoil true love, are you?'

'Surely, love depends upon honesty and trust.' Nicholas turned away from his brother to gaze out across the gardens of Whiteladies to the distant hills. 'You're deceiving Fanny, and it's wrong.'

'You can't jeopardise my marriage to Fanny without ruining my enterprise with Alfred Paslew,' remarked Theodore evenly. 'I'm not about to let that happen, Nick. I won't allow you to lose your nerve now.'

'I should've spoken out sooner!' the younger man muttered wretchedly.

'Take my advice, just as you always have,' Theodore replied easily. 'Let me do all the thinking. Be my best man in every respect and we'll all live happily ever after!'

Amy had shuddered as she'd watched and listened from the adjoining room. Despite the smoothness of his manner, there was undeniable menace behind Theodore's words.

He rose, pushing his brother towards the door that led out on to the landing. 'Go to your room and I'll see you at dinner. If you fancy a little sport afterwards, I'm going to The Mermaid for a few hands of cards. Monks Quay may be a desolate hole, but there's considerable wealth amongst the merchant classes in these little market towns.' His full mouth curved. 'I wager I'll soon hear the jingle of their purses...'

Nicholas left the room and the heavy oak door closed behind him.

Theodore turned towards the dresser to

pour himself another drink, and Amy waited a moment or two, ensuring the landing was clear before slipping from Gilbert Paslew's dressing-room. Theodore Buxton's fresh towels were still in her arms and quite forgotten about as, with pounding heart, she scurried along the landing towards the backstairs and fled to the safety of the kitchen.

Now, in the stillness of the summer night, Amy rubbed her throbbing temples with her fingertips. Slipping from the big bed, she moved across to the window and breathed deeply of the cool, clear, sea air.

Sitting on the oak chest, she tucked her knees beneath her chin and stared out into the darkness. Pa was out there somewhere, making his way homeward. Likely going into port at Liverpool before sailing the final miles back up to Monks Quay.

For a long while after their mother's death, the cottage had seemed unbearably empty whenever their father was away on the packet but, without even realising it, Amy and Fanny had grown accustomed to managing the household.

Rory, their eldest brother, however, despite being five years Amy's senior, was irresponsible and unreliable. Even Fanny's sharp tongue was becoming less and less effective at curbing his sullen wildness. And, in just a few days, Amy would have to cope with everything on her own.

The prospect weighed heavily upon her young shoulders. She lacked Fanny's brisk manner and self-assurance but, from now on, her younger siblings Vicky and Edmund – and Pa, too – would be depending upon her.

A chill breeze crept up into the room from the beach and Amy rose to fetch her shawl. The uneven floorboards creaked beneath her bare feet as she reached up to the hook beside Vicky's bed, and the child stirred.

'Is Pa home yet?'

'Shhh, it's still night,' whispered Amy, smoothing a stray strand of hair from her sister's forehead. 'Go back to sleep.'

'Will Pa be able to see his way home?' Vicky yawned, rubbing her eyes with her fists. 'Is the Dog Star shining?'

'It's shining brighter than all the other stars, just like always,' Amy said reassuringly, as Vicky's heavy eyelids fluttered closed once more. 'Lighting up the sea so Pa can sail home to us…'

Straightening up, Amy tiptoed from the bed.

'There's no need to creep!' Fanny's voice was crisp.

'I thought you were asleep.'

'I was,' returned Fanny, removing the muslin pads from her eyes before sitting up and pounding the pillows into a comfortable shape. 'I certainly hope–'

'Shhh,' mumbled Amy, climbing back into bed. 'Vicky's just gone off again!'

'I certainly hope Pa gets home promptly,' continued Fanny in a low voice. 'He was almost a week late coming back from his last trip.'

'That wasn't his fault! There was some problem with the Jenet Rae, you know that.'

'I also know I need a father to give me away!'

'I'm sure he'll be back in time. But you never can predict the weather and the seas.'

'Pa is skippering a packet up and down the coast, and back and forth to the Isle of Man and Ireland – not voyaging to the Americas!' retorted Fanny crossly, fussing with her ringlets. 'I just wish he hadn't sailed so close to my wedding day!'

'He can't refuse to sail!' protested Amy mildly, aware her sister was anxious the wedding be perfect. 'He couldn't afford to lose his wages for the trip and Mr Paslew

15

would probably sack him if he refused, anyway!'

'That wretched boat would make better time if Alfred Paslew would get it ship-shape!' went on Fanny. 'I know for a fact Pa's told him so. Paslew's willing enough to make a profit from the Jenet Rae, but he won't spend an extra shilling on her! It's not as if he can't afford it,' she concluded tartly. 'Paslew's the richest man in Monks Quay, and getting richer by the year. Mrs Ainsworth was telling me she heard he's just taken over the brick kilns at Hawridge and opened up an office in Lancaster!'

Amy drew breath to speak, then bit her tongue. How had Theodore described Alfred Paslew? A man whose greed knew no bounds? She hardly ever saw the master of the house while she was working at White-ladies Grange, but she was well aware that he had the reputation of being shrewd in business and dangerous to cross.

'When Pa gets back,' she said reflectively, 'it'll be the last day the family will all be together, won't it?'

'I hadn't thought about it, but yes, it will be.' Fanny exhaled a slow, contented breath. 'These are my last days as Miss Fanny MacFarlane! Oh, I can't wait to be married,

Amy! To be finally swept away from this suffocating little town and have a fine home of my own! Theo has told me so much about his house in Carteret Square. I feel as though I know every room already! And York is such a splendid city, so I'm told. We'll entertain, have dinner parties, go to concerts and to the theatre! I shall shop at only the finest establishments and wear beautiful clothes.'

She turned to Amy, her pretty face animated and her blue eyes sparkling.

'Theo and I are going to have such a wonderful life! It will be everything I've ever dreamed of!'

'I couldn't bear to go away from Monks Quay,' commented Amy softly. 'Won't you be even a little homesick?'

'I shall miss you and Pa and the children. Even Aunt Anne, despite her always fussing and disapproving of everything, but I'll scarcely miss Rory at all. He's always been surly and hot-headed, and he's grown worse of late. I fear he's fallen in with a rough crowd at the clay pits, Amy. You'll need to be careful, or he'll walk all over you. Our brother has taken it into his head that when Pa's away he can do whatever he pleases.' Her smooth brow creased. 'Unless he mends his ways, Rory will come to a very bad end indeed.'

Amy had scarcely been listening, her thoughts preoccupied with Fanny's rosy anticipation of her marriage.

'Fanny, how can you be – I mean, are you sure Theo is right for you? After all, just a year ago you'd never even met! And you haven't really spent much time together, have you?' she blurted out. 'We don't know much about him or his family. How can you be sure he's the man you want to spend the rest of your life with?'

'I knew Theo was the man for me from the moment we were introduced at that dreadful church social.' Fanny smiled, her eyes soft. 'And I've thanked my lucky stars every day since! I'm nearly twenty-three, Amy. I'd virtually given up hope of ever marrying and I was scared of being alone like Aunt Anne. At least she has her school but, without marriage, what would I have had? Whatever would have become of me?'

Amy was shocked. 'How could you ever have thought that way? You're beautiful! You could have had lots of suitors, if only you'd let them come calling!'

'Fishermen, ploughboys and shopkeepers. Dull as ditchwater and utterly lacking in ambition.' Fanny shook her head in exasperation, adding gently. 'You're like Ma, Amy! It means something to you that your family has lived here for generations. You love Clockmaker's Cottage and the shore, and the sea, and Monks Quay – but I don't. I've always felt so – so trapped! When Theo proposed it was like being set free, and suddenly I knew I didn't need to worry anymore and everything was going to be all right. You're still very young, Amy. You might not understand–'

'I do! I do, really,' she replied hastily. 'It's just... When I was at Whiteladies last evening, I overheard Theo and Nicholas talking. Well, arguing. Nicholas was saying ... it sounded as though ... that is, I don't think Theo has been honest with you, and–'

'Amy! That's quite enough!' interrupted Fanny sharply. 'You should not have been eavesdropping, and whatever you imagine you heard could not be of less interest to me. I believe I know my future husband rather better than you do, and I trust Theo completely. He's a perfect gentleman. I'm deeply hurt you should suggest otherwise!'

'Fanny, I'm so sorry! I didn't want to upset you! I only thought–'

'Theo and I are to be married, Amy,' cut

in Fanny. Reaching for the muslin pads, she lay down and covered her eyes once more. 'Please try to be happy for me.'

'I am...' Amy's voice trailed into silence. Then, although it was still very early, but being far too agitated to rest, she rose and began to dress.

Padding in her stockinged feet along the landing, past their parents' empty room and the smaller one next to it where her two brothers slept, Amy moved swiftly through the darkness and down the steep, crooked staircase into the stone-flagged kitchen. As soon as she lit the lamp, she saw that the cold supper of bread, cheese and pickled onion that she'd left out for Rory was still untouched on the sideboard.

Getting down on her knees, she began raking out the warm ashes and setting the fire, frowning while she worked.

When she'd arrived home from White-ladies last evening, Rory had already been home from the clay pits and, according to Fanny, had gone straight out again without waiting for his meal. Hence the cold supper. Where could he have been heading in such a rush? The Green Man, probably, Amy reasoned dismally. The Green Man was a rough tavern on the outskirts of Monks Quay, and much frequented by the clay pit men.

Of course, it was possible that Rory had come home so late that he'd gone up to bed without eating anything. But a glance at the back of the door, from where Rory's coat was missing, proved that it wasn't so.

Amy was worried. He'd never stayed out the whole night before.

Gently wafting the fire into life so that it wouldn't smoke, Amy put together the makings of breakfast before starting upstairs again.

Pushing open the door of her brothers' room, she could make out the shape of Rory's narrow bed, flat and unoccupied.

'Amy? Is that you?' Edmund's voice was low. 'I've been awake for ages. Where's Rory? He hasn't been in all night.'

'I know, Eddy,' she replied. 'Did he say anything when he got home from the clay pits last night? Where was he going? What was he doing?'

Edmund grinned. 'Rory doesn't tell me anything!'

Amy nodded.

There was almost seven years between the brothers, and about all they had in common was their family name.

'I've lit the fire and started breakfast, but it's far too early to serve it up.'

She glanced through the small-paned window before turning from the room.

'Rory's due at the clay pits in a couple of hours or so. He'll be put on notice if he's late again.'

Following her downstairs, Edmund hesitated before speaking.

'He'll be sacked, Amy. Charlie Thorpe at school told me – his brother works at the clay pits – Charlie told me old Bostock, the overseer, put Rory on notice a couple of weeks ago for talking back. Charlie said Bostock is really strict, and Rory was lucky not to be sacked on the spot.'

'Eddy! Why didn't you tell Fanny and me about this?'

Edmund shrugged uncomfortably. 'I couldn't, Amy! I couldn't tell tales – where are you going?'

'To find Rory – if he loses his job, word will get around that he's unreliable and no one else will take him on.'

'I'll come with you–'

'No, stay here. I'll be fine, Eddy. I'll take the light.'

Touching a flame to the lantern, Amy let herself out into the chill, dark morning.

Her footsteps were silenced by the coarse sand as, swinging the lantern from side to side to cast its beam wide lest Rory had passed out in his cups on the track leading home, she swiftly left Clockmaker's Cottage behind her and started the steep walk up towards the town.

The rough track presently became cobbles, and soon Amy passed by Aunt Anne's schoolhouse, then continued on around All Hallows church into the market square.

Pausing beneath the ancient market cross, her gaze swept the dark streets and buildings, trying to penetrate the great wells of blackness yawning beyond every archway, ginnel, and narrow twisting lane.

Rory might be anywhere!

He could be hurt, and lying somewhere in the deserted town or down by the quayside. He could be up in the hills, where the scars of Paslew's clay workings showed pale, or he could be lying amongst the dunes, or on the shore. Perhaps he'd stayed the night with a workmate in one of the ramshackle terraces of mean dwellings that the clay pits and quarry had spawned. If that were so, she'd never find him!

Hopeless as it seemed, Amy raised the

lantern once more and, looking in doorways and along alleys as she went, began walking. She had stepped on to the town's main thoroughfare and had gone just a few hundred yards along Abbotsgate when the glowing lights of The Mermaid came into sight and she heard the whicker and stamp of horses as she approached the coaching inn's neat and tidy yard.

Brisk footsteps rang out on the cobbles, and Amy jumped when a low voice hailed her from the shadows.

'Amy? Amy MacFarlane?' The footsteps quickened and a broad-shouldered figure strode from The Mermaid's yard. 'Whatever are you doing in the town at this hour. Is something wrong? Is it the packet...?'

'No! No, Dan. Nothing like that. It's...' She faltered, reluctant to speak of family troubles even with somebody she'd known since schooldays. 'It's Rory. He didn't come home last night.'

'Your brother's a grown man,' returned Dan Ainsworth stiffly, shifting the weight of the harness slung across his shoulder. 'You shouldn't be out in the pitch-dark looking for him.'

'I think he might've gone to The Green Man. He probably got drunk,' she mumbled, shamefaced. 'He'll lose his job if he doesn't turn up to the clay pits on time.'

'I'll help you look…'

'I can manage, Dan!' she cut in. 'You have work to do. You've to be ready for the first coach.'

'There's time enough yet – and even if there weren't, I'd not let you go wandering around Monks Quay searching for a drunkard!'

Dan turned on his heel towards the stables.

'Let me fetch a light and we'll be on our way. Don't fret, lass,' he added over his shoulder. 'Rory's got sharp wits and a hard head; he'll not have come to any great harm!'

All Hallows' clock was striking the quarter-hour as they proceeded along Abbotsgate in the direction of The Green Man, with Amy keeping a sharp look-out to one side and Dan to the other. Their footsteps were loud upon the steep street and seemed the only sounds in the whole town.

'This is kind of you, Dan,' she murmured after a while. 'I appreciate it more than you know. Rory's got into bad company at the clay pits.'

'Don't make excuses for him! It's a dis-

25

grace, him carrying-on the way he does. He should be taking care of his family when your da is away, not having his sister run herself ragged because he can't hold his ale!'

'I know you're right. Rory seems only to care for himself, but I do worry about him. I can't help it.'

'Aye, you always were a soft-hearted one! Even as a little lass.' He smiled across at her adding with a frown, 'And I reckon you may have cause to be concerned.'

'What's happened?' she demanded, the knot of anxiety tightening within her.

'Maybe nothing.' He shrugged. 'I don't know anything for sure.'

'You live in town, Dan! You know what's going on. At The Mermaid, you're bound to see things. Hear things.' She spoke rapidly, turning to him. 'You must tell me!'

'I don't know what Rory's up to, Amy, and that's the truth.'

They fell silent as they passed by Ged Beresford's workshop. A finished coffin still stood on the carpenter's saw-horses in readiness for the burial of Mary Pearson, who'd been lost in childbirth, and her babe.

'Fanny's intended and his brother were in The Mermaid last night,' continued Dan after a while. 'Being market day, the place was packed to the rafters and they were playing cards with Collie Barraclough and a few other regulars. It was late, and I was surprised when I saw Rory walk in – he never comes into The Mermaid. He always does his drinking out at The Green Man, and last night he'd already had a fair few from the looks of him. Anyhow, next thing, the younger Buxton brother was standing out of the game and Rory was at the table playing in his stead. For high stakes, too.'

'Rory was gambling?' Her face fell. 'Pa would be furious if he found out! How could he afford to – oh, no – he got paid yesterday!'

'Aye, I guessed as much. It was all over pretty quick. Rory was outclassed – Buxton's a sharp player. Better than he chooses to show, I fancy,' commented Dan matter-of-factly. 'Last I saw of Rory, he was sat in the parlour with Buxton, talking real close over a smoke and a couple of whiskies. I went for another barrel, and when I came back up both the brothers were at the card table again and Rory was gone.'

'He'd lost all his wages, yet he didn't come home,' pondered Amy, trying to make sense of it. 'Where is he? And why would he go to The Mermaid in the first place? Rory's scarcely been civil to Theo on the few occasions they've met, so what could they have been talking about?'

The Green Man stood just ahead of them, and they walked all around the dilapidated tavern with its broken roofs and boarded-up windows without luck. Finally turning towards the town once more, Dan suddenly veered away from Abbotsgate.

'He was already drunk. He'd lost his wages playing cards,' he muttered. 'There's one place Rory might've gone to lick his wounds.'

'Where are we going?' exclaimed Amy, running to keep up with him as he strode through a maze of squalid alleys crammed with mean dwellings. She almost fell over a woman curled up and snoring against some railings.

'I've never been here before!'

'I should hope not!' Dan returned drily, all the time shining the light and searching. 'Look into the doorways and corners, Amy.'

They'd scarcely gone twenty yards into the depths of Tanners Row, with Dan glancing down each set of stone steps to the cellars of the squalid buildings, when he spotted something and raised the lantern for a better look. 'Amy over here!'

Immediately at his side, Amy pressed her

hand to her mouth to stifle the cry. In the lantern's guttering light, she could just make out a crumpled figure sprawled upon the cobbles close to a midden wall. Before Dan could hold her back, she was on her knees at Rory's side. Fearfully, she touched a hand to his cold skin, gently smoothing back the blood-matted hair from his face – this time unable to prevent a cry of anguish from escaping her lips.

'He's not dead, lass,' said Dan briskly, drawing Amy to her feet. 'Dead drunk is what he is!'

'But look at his face! And his hands!' She took one of Rory's rough, grimy hands in her own. 'He's cut and bleeding – he's been attacked, hasn't he?'

'Fighting, I'd say. And gave as good as he got! I'd not care to see the other bloke,' re-marked Dan, noting the grazes and bruising on Rory's fists and knuckles.

Rory MacFarlane was fast getting a name around Monks Quay for trouble-making and being too quick with his fists – but there was no need for Amy to know that.

Not before she had to, at any rate.

'We'll get him back to The Mermaid and sober him up,' grunted Dan, bending to lift the inert figure. 'He'll get to the clay pits in time whether he likes it or not!'

It was a long walk down Abbotsgate, back to the inn. Rory didn't stir as Dan half-carried and half-dragged him along, finally propping him against the horse trough in The Mermaid's yard.

'Are you sure he'll be all right?' fretted Amy, her fingertips gently touching Rory's swollen cheekbone and bloody jaw. 'I'll bathe his face–'

'You'll do no such thing! You're worn out and chilled to the bone – go inside to the fire and get yourself some hot tea. I'll see to Sleeping Beauty.' Dan filled a bucket from the water pump. 'He'll be in a foul mood when he comes to, so don't expect any thanks!'

Amy did as she was bidden, grateful for the warmth and respite.

She'd never actually been inside The Mermaid Inn before, even though it was a perfectly respectable establishment with a fine reputation for good food and hospitality.

The inn had been in Dan Ainsworth's family for generations and was host to merchants, traders and ladies and gentlemen in coaches from all over the country and much farther afield, as well as local folk.

Presently, Dan called her out to the stable yard, where she found Rory, dripping wet and scowling, leaning back against the mounting block.

'Are you all right?'

'What the blazes are you doing here?'

He glowered up at her as he staggered to his feet, then reeled and stumbled back to the ground.

'Don't just stand there, girl! Help me up!'

However, even as Amy moved towards him, Rory lashed out and shoved her aside. Rolling clumsily to his left, he struggled to remove his boot and tipped out a heavy purse. Using his teeth to wrench open the drawstrings, he emptied the contents into the palm of his cupped hand.

Amy gasped. She'd never seen so much money!

'Nowt to do with you!' he hissed, replacing his boot and scrambling to his feet. 'Keep quiet about it or you'll be sorry!'

Dan Ainsworth stepped between brother and sister. 'Watch that temper, Rory!'

'Out of my way!' He squared up to Dan. 'What I said to her goes double for you!'

'Ah, don't make an even bigger fool of yourself.'

Dan turned away, and in that instant Rory lunged at him.

A scream choked in Amy's throat as the two men crashed to the ground, rolling over and over on the cobbled yard. But Dan Ainsworth was the stronger and managed to overpower Rory, hauling him to his feet and pushing him back against the inn's wall.

'Get yourself along to the clay pits,' he muttered, breathing hard. 'And be glad you've still a job to go to!'

'Go to hell!' Rory spat blood, striding across the stable yard without a backward glance. 'Go to hell, the pair of you!'

He passed through the archway into Abbotsgate and was gone from their sight.

Suddenly, Amy was trembling violently. Rory had always been hot-headed, but this...

'He'll have calmed down by the time he gets to the pits,' reassured Dan, moving to her side. 'And I wouldn't pay any heed to his threats. It's last night's ale talking. I'll fetch the wagon and drive you home.

The sun was rising as Dan harnessed the stocky, brown horse, and the wagon trundled out through the archway into Abbotsgate. The market town was soon left behind and the rattled on westwards between the fields until reaching the rough shore track leading to Clockmaker's Cottage.

Amy glanced back at the distant spirals of smoke rising from the chimneys of Monks Quay. What on earth had Rory been doing in town last night? However had he come by so much money?

She was cold with fear for the trouble he might have got himself into. And trouble it must surely be for Rory to have possession of so many sovereigns.

A Happy Day!

Amy was sitting in the bay window at the far end of the south-facing landing at Whiteladies Grange, making the most of the clear afternoon light.

Her days at Whiteladies were settled into a not unpleasant routine, and these hours after luncheon and before tea, when the housework was done and she was dressed in her black dress and frilled white cap and apron so as to be presentable above stairs, were her favourite time. She'd taken her sewing basket and a bundle of mending into the widow seat and, as soon as a cigar burn in a damask table cloth had been invisibly repaired, Amy took out her coloured silks and picked up the runner she was embroidering for the youngest Paslew daughter.

So engrossed was she in her work that she was unaware of Eleanor Paslew approaching along the landing and, startled, jabbed herself with the needle when the tall, angular woman spoke to her.

Amy was on her feet at once and bobbing a polite curtsey.

'Oh! I do beg your pardon, ma'am! I didn't hear–'

'That's quite all right, Amy. Do carry on with your sewing.' Mrs Paslew smiled, sitting beside her on the window seat. 'How are you settling in at Whiteladies?'

'Everybody's been very kind to me, ma'am,' the girl replied. 'I – I like working here very much.'

'I'm pleased to hear it. Mrs Braithwaite tells me you perform your duties diligently, are always willing, and have a good memory for your chores.'

'I write down a lot of the things Mrs Braithwaite tells me to do,' began Amy, and at once bit her tongue, wondering if she'd spoken out of turn.

Hadn't Fanny warned her that many employers didn't like their servants to be able to read and write?

'It helps me to remember, ma'am. Is that all right?'

'Indeed it is.' The warmth of Mrs Paslew's smile reached her eyes, transforming her plain face. 'I would expect nothing less than perfect literacy from a niece and former pupil of Anne Shawcross! How is your aunt,

Amy? Apart from church, I'm afraid I hardly ever see her now. Yet we were great friends when young; did you know that?'

Amy's soft brown eyes glanced up fleetingly from her needlework.

'No, ma'am.'

'We were in the choir together at All Hallows. My father was vicar at that time. I knew your dear mother, too, of course,' added Mrs Paslew gently, 'although not so very well, because Caroline was considerably younger than Anne and I.'

Amy nodded, unsure of what to say. Apart from during her interview for her position at Whiteladies, Amy hadn't had occasion to speak to Eleanor Paslew at all. Suddenly, she realised the mistress was watching her keenly as she sewed.

'May I see?' Mrs Paslew extended a slender hand and spread the creamy embroidered linen across her lap, examining the needlework depicting an ornate little gate set into the corner of a walled garden filled with flowers.

'When I asked you to make a runner for Clementine's dresser, and that you might choose the design, I had in mind a simple pattern of decorative edging. It never occurred to me you would attempt anything so elaborate!'

Amy was flustered; worried she'd over-stepped her place.

'I'm sorry, ma'am. It's just, well, while I was thinking about which stitches and patterns to use, I saw Miss Clementine sitting reading in the walled garden beside the gate and so...' her voice trailed off. She just couldn't afford to lose her job at White-ladies! 'I'm really sorry, ma'am. I haven't opened any new silks from the box. I've only used up ones already open and–'

'That's of no concern, child. You must use whatever materials you require,' Mrs Paslew interrupted. 'That particular corner of the walled garden has been Clementine's favourite place since she was a very small child. To portray it on her runner was thoughtful, and I'm certain Clementine will be delighted. It's beautiful work, Amy.'

'Thank you, ma'am. Ma was a fine needlewoman and she taught both Fanny and I, but Fanny is much better than me.'

'You've drawn the design cleverly,' went on Mrs Paslew, studying the girl's animated face. 'Can you tell me the names of the stitches you're using?'

'They're all quite simple ones really,' responded Amy, her shyness melting as she

37

smoothed out the linen cloth. 'Stem stitches for the flower stalks and some of the leaves. Satin stitch for the fuller, bigger leaves here and here. Daisy stitch, long and short stitch, and straight stitches for all the flowers. French knots for the buds, and thicker satin stitches in the gate, garden wall and for the little bird on the branch – although I haven't started her yet!'

'You don't use a hoop, even though there is one in the box?'

'I can work this pattern better without one, ma'am.'

'I see. Well, if you require anything that isn't in the sewing box, you must say so and it shall be ordered for you from the haberdasher in Liverpool. Do you understand?'

'Yes, ma'am.'

'I have an idea that when my other daughters see Clementine's new runner, you'll be kept busy sewing for them, too. Will you mind that, Amy?'

'Oh, no! I love sewing. Especially fancy, pretty things like this.'

'I must have a word with Mrs Braithwaite so that you may be allowed a little more time for needlework. The drawing-room would benefit from new cushions, I fancy!' She rose from the widow seat. 'Is your father ashore at present?'

'No, ma'am. Pa's due home with the tide early this evening.'

'Ah, yes. I recall Mr Paslew mentioning the packet was returning today. I daresay there's much for you to do at home in readiness for tomorrow's celebrations?'

'Aunt Anne's helped us with the dressmaking and the cooking. She's done ever so much baking.'

'That sounds like Anne! I'm sure it will be a wonderful wedding. Your sister and Theodore make a charming couple. It's been a delight having him and Nicholas staying with us and Gilbert's home from university at last. I do like it when this old house is lively and filled with young people!'

Eleanor Paslew turned and started along the wide landing.

'Be sure to go into the kitchen and see Mrs Braithwaite before you leave this evening, won't you, Amy?' she called back.

'Yes, ma'am,' Amy replied, hoping against hope that Gladys Braithwaite wouldn't have a long list of chores for her to complete before she could go for the night!

As soon as the light began to fade, she tidied away the sewing box and dutifully went downstairs into the kitchen.

'Will there be anything else, Mrs Braith-waite?'

'Nowt that won't wait till you come up first thing in the morning, lass,' replied Gladys Braithwaite, looking up from her pastry-making. 'Maisie, fetch that hamper from the pantry – and don't trail sand all across my clean floor while you're doing it!' she called to a thin-faced girl who was sanding pans at the sink. 'The missus asked me to put up a few treats for the marriage feast,' she went on to Amy, as the scullery maid returned with a large basket. 'There are pies, potted meats and suchlike; a big tipsy cake and some fruit jellies. And I put in a couple of my special mulled puddings for good measure. One's for eating after the wedding and the other's to keep for the birth of their first child.'

'How thoughtful!' exclaimed Amy, raising the linen cloth and peeking into the laden basket. 'Fanny will be delighted – she's on pins that tomorrow should be really special for everyone!'

'It'll be special in more ways than one,' remarked Mrs Braithwaite sagely. 'Likely the last time the MacFarlanes'll be together. Nothing will be the same once Fanny's wed and gone.'

'She'll only be in York, Mrs Braithwaite!' protested Amy, more cheerfully than she felt. 'Theodore's family home is near the Minster. In Carteret Square.'

'Never heard of it, nor been there,' returned the old woman, her plump fingers deftly decorating the pastry crusts with scallops and twists. 'But if you can't walk it, that makes it far enough away for you to lose touch! A shame Mr Buxton won't have any family of his own at his wedding, isn't it?' she went on casually, glancing sidelong at Amy. 'Apart from his brother standing beside him, of course. Unusual, too. Folk of quality generally have hoards of kith and kin turning up at their weddings, don't they?'

'Mr Buxton – Theodore – lost his father last year. The family are still in mourning. Lavish celebrations wouldn't have been appropriate, Mrs Braithwaite,' replied Amy stiffly.

As well as cooking for and managing the household at Whiteladies Grange, Gladys Braithwaite kept busy by gossiping and prying into other folks' affairs.

Crossing her fingers firmly behind her back, Amy added, 'Besides, Fanny wanted a quiet wedding.'

'Would've thought a big society do would

be more to your Fanny's taste!' said the cook, sniffily. 'She always has such a fine air about her.'

'Everyone says she's done right well for herself catching the likes of Mr Buxton,' chipped in Maisie unexpectedly, looking up from her pans. 'Him being a gentleman and all, and her just a common seafarer's daughter!'

'I think Fanny and Theo are both very lucky to have found each other,' Amy said with a smile to the little scullery maid.

Maisie was but eleven or twelve years old and Amy realised the girl was only repeating comments she'd heard from her elders. Gladys Braithwaite doubtless amongst them. Picking up the hamper with a struggle, Amy started from the kitchen.

'Goodnight – see you in the morning!'

Swiftly changing from her black dress into her own clothes and wrapping a shawl about her shoulders, Amy lost no time scurrying across the drying green and around the tall yew hedge, away from the house – only to collide with Nicholas Buxton, who was standing in the middle of the path, staring towards the hills.

'Oh!'

'I do beg your pardon!' he apologised at

once, reaching out to steady her. 'I'm most awfully sorry, Amy!'

'My fault, Mr Nicholas!' she replied, balancing the hamper on her hip, straightening her hat and managing to bob a curtsey all at once. 'I wasn't looking where I was going.'

'Nonsense! You weren't expecting to turn the corner and find some melancholy fool blocking your path! And, Amy, can't you please call me Nicholas – or Nick, even? After all, this time tomorrow we will be family!'

She smiled up at him. From the little she knew of the Buxton brothers, they could hardly have been more different in temperament as well as appearance.

Theodore was tall and muscular with features almost as dark as a gypsy's, whereas Nicholas was slightly built, pale of countenance and reddish-haired.

The starkest contrast was between the brothers' characters, however, the younger being mild-mannered, shy almost, and the elder urbane and somehow unprincipled.

Their acrimonious argument of the previous evening flashed vividly into Amy's thoughts, her disquiet clearly revealed upon her expressive face.

'Are you all right?' Nicholas queried at

once, taking the heavy hamper from her arms. 'Let me carry this. Are you on your way home?'

'Yes, but I can manage. Really,' she protested. 'It's not far. I take the short-cut through Friars Wood and across–'

'Then I'll walk with you,' he interrupted gently. 'Truth to tell, Amy, I'll be glad of your company. I'm weary of being alone with my thoughts.'

A rather awkward silence lengthened between them as they crossed the park from Whiteladies Grange and walked down towards the wood with its old trees and fresh green foliage.

Amy was racking her brains for something to say, when Nicholas gestured expansively towards the cloudless sky and surrounding landscape.

'Thank goodness the weather's been fine today!' he exclaimed. 'There's little worse than a cold wet picnic, and the weather looked far from promising when Theo set off to collect Fanny.'

'I didn't know they were going out today.'

'Spur of the moment thing, I think,' he went on. 'We were out riding this morning and Theo asked Gilbert to recommend a pleasing place for a picnic. He immediately mentioned a place called St Agnes Falls. Said it was beautiful. Incredibly beautiful and tranquil, were his exact words! Do you know it?'

'Mmm. Ma used to take us there sometimes when we were small. It is lovely. Especially at this time of year,' she replied, rather surprised that someone like Gilbert Paslew would even be aware of such an out of the way spot. 'There's a dell beneath the falls that's filled with flowers all summer long.'

'According to Gilbert, there are some quite rare plants and grasses that grow there,' went on Nicholas. 'He was telling us something about a holy spring from ancient times. Long ago monks were travelling through Lancashire and they stopped for the night in the woods. At dawn they saw a vision at the spring and that was why they decided to establish their monastery here in Monks Quay. Then the nuns came, and Whiteladies Grange was built. Although it wasn't called Whiteladies Grange in those days of course.'

'I didn't know any of that!' exclaimed Amy. 'I've never heard that story. How wonderful!'

'Oh, Gilbert knows all sorts of things. He's a frightfully clever chap. Always was. He used to help me with my prep at school, and Gilbert had this odd way of making even really boring things like theology and philosophy seem quite lively. I muddled through, thanks to him.'

Nicholas grinned at her as they clambered over the stile into Friars Wood.

'I'm pretty much a duffer – Theo has the brains in our family!'

'I enjoyed school – my Aunt Anne is the teacher here – and I do like learning things, but Edmund's the clever one in our family. He's always studying and hopes to get a scholarship to a good school,' said Amy. 'Did you go to boarding school, Nicholas?'

'Oh, yes. Father was posted to India as a very young man, and that's where he met and married my mother. She was from an army family, too. Neither one of them set foot on English soil for more than thirty years. I doubt very much if Mother will ever make the journey now. She's not strong, and since Father died...' He smiled sadly. 'India and the regiment have been my mother's whole life. Her friends and home are there.'

'It must've been very hard to leave your parents to come to school in a strange country,' Amy remarked sympathetically. 'I couldn't bear the thought of leaving my family and home!'

'It's not the done thing to own up to, but I was pretty miserable as a boy,' conceded Nicholas. 'I mean, Theo's the best brother anybody could wish for and he did his best to look out for me – it's always been Theo and me against the world – but because he was eight years my senior, we weren't able to see much of each other during term-time. Holidays were all right. We spent those together at the school, with other boys whose folk were abroad.'

'You didn't go home to India at all? It must've been such a lonely life!'

'Oh, it wasn't so bad. Just the way things are, I suppose,' he answered brightly. 'Although everything bucked up no end once I got to know Gilbert. He's a fine friend. The Paslews started inviting me to spend vacations with them at Whiteladies – Theo had long since left school and was back in India with the diplomatic corps by then. Even after we grew up and Gil went to Oxford, he and I remained the best of pals.'

'Last summer, when Theo met Fanny,' ventured Amy, 'was that the first time he'd been to Whiteladies?'

'Yes. Yes, it was.' Nicholas gazed straight ahead, beyond the meadows and down to the shimmering ribbon of sea. 'We had a wonderful visit and, as you know, were invited back for Christmas and the New Year. Theo and Mr Paslew get on like a house on fire,' he concluded, a frown creasing his forehead. 'Things in common, I suppose. Business and suchlike. They talk together for hours on end. Amy?'– He met her eyes as they passed through the back gate of Clockmaker's Cottage and walked up through the garden towards the kitchen door– 'Have you ever done something and later wished you hadn't? And – and then not done something you know full well you should've done to put it right? Then suddenly it's too late and you've done nothing to stop it and set things to right? No!' He looked distractedly away from her, his voice dropping. 'No, of course you haven't. Only I could be such a fool–'

'You're back!' Vicky burst from the cottage and hurtled towards them. 'What's in the big basket, Amy? What is it? Is it for Fanny's wedding? Can I see?'

'Not until Fanny gets home,' replied Amy.

She bent to hug her young sister, but her gaze never left Nicholas Buxton's face as he stepped into the cool larder and set down the wedding hamper.

'Nicholas–'

'I'd best be off.' He forced a smile, tipping his hat and moving out into the garden once more. 'I shouldn't have... Just ignore me! Theo often tells me I fuss and fume too much over things, and I'm sure he's right!'

'Please,' she persisted quietly, walking with him to the gate. 'Won't you at least come in for a cup of tea?'

He shook his head and smiled down at her.

'Best be getting back. Thank you for our walk, Amy. I enjoyed it. And our conversation.'

'I did, too...' Even as the words left her lips, Nicholas Buxton was walking up through the meadows towards Friars Wood, leaving Amy filled with questions, while Vicky tugged at her skirts and dragged at her hands.

'Aunt Anne's ironing my dress for tomorrow, and we've made cherry biscuits – I cut them out myself!' The little girl broke free, running on ahead. 'Come and see! Hurry!'

Amy dutifully followed, pausing at the apple tree where Edmund – unnoticed by Nicholas – was sitting reading.

He looked up from his book. 'What was all that about with Nicholas Buxton?'

Amy sighed, staring indoors. 'I only wish I knew.'

The Monks Quay packet was due home on the evening tide, and Vicky was up in the sisters' room, watching from under the eaves for the first glimpse of Pa's boat on the horizon. Amy and Aunt Anne were in the cottage's comfortable sitting-room, winding wool and relishing the peace.

'We should get that clock parcelled up tonight,' commented Anne Shawcross, nodding at the fine walnut corner clock made by her great-grandfather as a wedding gift for his bride.

Shawcrosses had made clocks in that very room since the 1690s, the craft being passed from father to son, down the years until Anne's generation, when only daughters had been born to the family. Then a century and more of skill and tradition died and was buried with their father.

'There won't be time to fuss with it tomorrow.'

'I wish Ma was here to pass the clock on to Fanny,' mused Amy. 'That clock always reminds me of Ma. She loved it so.'

'I love it too,' admitted Anne unexpectedly. 'Caroline and I grew up with its tick and chime – and Father made such a ceremony of winding it up each night on his way to bed! After your grandparents died and your mother and I were living here alone, I'd sometimes sit in this room just listening to the clock – imagining all the years and the lives and the faces it has seen passing. I was still quite young then,' she finished briskly, 'with a fair share of fanciful notions!'

'You love this cottage, don't you, Aunt Anne?' remarked Amy softly. 'Every bit as much as I do.'

'I was born and grew up here. All my happy memories are within these walls,' she answered simply. 'Although I haven't lived here for more than twenty years, I suppose I still think of Clockmaker's Cottage as home.'

'It must've broken your heart to leave it and move into the schoolhouse!'

'Don't be melodramatic, child!' Anne shook her head, tying off a bobbin. 'Caroline had a husband, and a baby on the way. It was only right and proper that her family should have the cottage to themselves. Especially since the school had its own house standing empty on its doorstep! No more treks back and forth into town for me. It was far more convenient all around. Vicky's very quiet isn't she? I'd better see what she's up to.'

'I'll go–' Amy rose, just as there was a

51

shriek from above and Vicky clattered down the steep stairs.

'Is it Pa's boat?'

'No. It's only Fanny and Theodore approaching in the carriage, but Amy!' She screwed up her face, thinking. 'Amy, I've waited and waited for Pa to come and he hasn't. I don't think he can find his way home!'

'Of course he can, pet!' exclaimed Amy with a smile. 'Why wouldn't he?'

'Because it's daylight!' persisted Vicky. 'There aren't any stars, are there? If the Dog Star's not shining, then Pa won't know which way to sail, will he?'

Aunt Anne cast an I-told-you-so glance at Amy, who was lost for words.

Amy's fairy-story, about the big bright Dog Star lighting up the sky so Pa could see his way home at night had soothed Vicky's bedtime fears about her father getting lost at sea in the dark. The comforting tale had done the trick. And it had seemed such a good idea at the time...

'Vicky, Pa doesn't need the Dog Star when it's still light like this. Now, you know how much he likes asparagus? Shall we gather some for his homecoming supper?'

'Dog Star, indeed!' tutted Aunt Anne,

peering over her spectacles at Amy when Vicky had gone to look for her boots. 'That child is going to grow up with a distorted view of the natural world – just you mark my words!'

Ramsay MacFarlane was at home safe and sound and the table set for supper when Rory came in, looking as if he had indeed spent that day working up at Paslew's clay pits.

'A scrap with a bloke at the pits,' he said dismissively in answer to his father's questions about his bruised and swollen face as he settled down to his meal. 'Summat and nowt.'

'You're not a lad any more, Rory. It's high time you grew up and started using your brain instead of your fists,' was all Ramsay said on the matter, but Amy knew full well it was only because he didn't want to spoil the happy occasion of the family's home-coming supper.

Straight after the meal, Rory snatched up his coat and strode out again. It wasn't until the dishes were cleared and washed; Vicky tucked up and asleep; Edmund studying; Fanny mixing honey and fine oatmeal into a concoction for her face; and Aunt Anne had returned to the schoolhouse, that Ramsay went out into the garden and gathered an armful of summer flowers.

'Amy – I'm off to see your ma.'

'Mind if I come?' She smiled at him already untying her apron. 'I'll just fetch my bonnet...'

The quarter-moon was rising above them as they turned their backs upon the sea and started towards All Hallows, its square bell-tower and surmounting cross silhouetted against the velvety night sky. It was the first chance they'd had to talk alone.

'Was everything all right this voyage, Pa? With the Jenet Rae?'

'She needs repair, Amy. A boat's like a living thing. It needs proper looking after, and Alfred Paslew just doesn't care, that's the truth of it.' Ramsay weighed his words. 'The Jenet Rae isn't as seaworthy as she should be, lass. If we hit bad weather she could get into difficulties. I told Paslew as much after the last voyage, and the one before that, but all he cares about is a quick profit. He's not a seaman and he's got no interest in the packet. Never had, and never will.'

Amy shook her head, perplexed. 'So, why did he bother buying her?'

'Because the Jenet Rae is another piece of Monks Quay for him to own!' returned Ramsay tersely. 'After old Spencer died, his widow didn't want the boat or the business. The poor woman just wanted shot of the whole caboodle and enough money to move away to live with her daughter in Douglas. Paslew saw the chance of a bargain and he snapped it up. He won't be satisfied till he owns the whole town, and everyone in it!'

They reached the lychgate of All Hallows and Ramsay removed his hat as they walked the winding path towards the church.

'I'm truly glad Fanny's getting married, and I hope she'll be very happy,' murmured Amy, slipping her arm through her father's. 'I just wish she was staying here with us in Monks Quay instead of going so far away.'

'A wife's place is with her husband, Amy. Theo's not our class. He belongs to a different world. There's nothing here for him. I did have my doubts about him and Fanny at first, but they look a good match and Fanny never would've been happy wed to a local lad and living in Monks Quay, you know.'

'I suppose not.' She smiled as they neared the west door of the church.

Ma rested across the churchyard in the far corner beneath the willows. Pa always visited her as soon as he got home from the sea.

'I'll go inside to wait for you.'

'Thanks, lass.' He kissed her forehead. 'I'll not be long.'

She watched his figure receding into the soft summer darkness before she stepped inside the porch.

Her hand was upon the round door handle when the sound of voices within the church caused her to hesitate. If Reverend Linley was speaking with a parishioner, she didn't wish to intrude.

Booted footsteps approached the door, scraping on the stone-flagged nave, and as the voices of two men drew nearer and more distinct, Amy recognised both.

Rory and Theodore Buxton!

The handle turned from inside and she shrank back into the deep shadows, her heart hammering. The heavy door was pulled open and the men emerged, striding across the porch. Clearly they had concluded their conversation within the sacred confines of the church, for not another word passed between them.

Descending the steps, they each went their separate ways. Theodore Buxton towards the east gate, where a bridle path led through the woods to Whiteladies Grange, and Rory vanishing swiftly into the night in the direction of The Green Man tavern.

It was a beautiful wedding, everyone said so. After the register had been signed, the bells had been rung, and the rice and rose petals thrown, the newly-weds drove in the Paslews' carriage down to Clockmaker's Cottage with their guests following on foot, horseback and cart.

The summer's afternoon was fine and warm so the wedding feast was set out in the garden, where the happy couple were toasted and well-wished with ale and cider gifted by the Ainsworth family, or fruit cordial from Aunt Anne's kitchen.

Amy wasn't sure if Pa had given Rory a good talking-to, but her brother had been on his best behaviour all day. He'd been polite and amiable to everybody and had even borrowed a penny whistle to join in with the fiddlers, flute and squeeze-box players providing reels and jigs for the dancing.

Folk who weren't dancing were drifting about the garden drinking and chatting.

It had been a lovely day, reflected Amy from her quiet seat beneath the apple tree. Fanny had never looked more radiant, nor Pa so proud! Ma would've–

'A penny for them!'

She started, squinting up through the dappled sunlight to find Dan Ainsworth beaming down at her.

'I was remembering past times.' She smiled, gazing wistfully around her mother's garden. 'It's funny how things from long ago can seem so close!'

'I know exactly what you mean.' Steadying his tankard of ale, Dan dropped to his knees, stretching out on the grass at Amy's feet. 'I remember Uncle Bruce sailing in from America like it was yesterday! I was only a little lad yet I can recall all his tales about being a newspaperman in New York and Chicago. I don't suppose you remember my Uncle Bruce, do you?'

She shook her head. It was peculiar. Since they'd left school, she and Dan Ainsworth had merely exchanged pleasantries whenever they met in the town yet now it was somehow as if they were the closest of friends.

'Do you still want to be a newspaperman like your uncle?'

'Why, Amy! It's years ago I told you that! I'm amazed you remember!' He grinned, teasing her. 'It was when we were sat together on the back row of your Aunt Anne's school room, wasn't it?'

58

She lowered her eyes, glancing away to where Pa was taking his turn at throwing horseshoes.

'It was on our last day at school, and Aunt Anne asked us to write an essay about what we'd most like to do with our lives,' Amy said, meeting his gaze with a smile. 'You were always really good at writing.'

'Much good it's done me so far!' He sighed. 'But aye, I'd still like to be a newspaperman. Da's all for me taking over The Mermaid one day, just like he did from his da. That's the trouble with small towns like Monks Quay, you know. You're brought up to do exactly what your father did before you – whether you like it or not!'

'And you don't like it?'

He swirled the ale around his tankard, considering.

'It's not that, exactly. It's just that I reckon I'd be good at writing for a newspaper, given half a chance. And it's not like I'm the only son, is it? Amos or Sam could just as easy run The Mermaid when they're old enough.'

'Would you sail to America, like your uncle did?'

'Maybe. I'd like to go to all the places he writes to me about.'

He paused, watching a ladybird settle

59

momentarily upon the toe of Amy's satin slipper before fluttering away.

'I see the ocean every day of my life. I look out across all that water and think there's a whole world out there. I want to see some of it before I die.'

'You sound just like Fanny! She always wanted to get away,' said Amy softly. 'I look across the sea, too – but I've never ever wanted to sail away! This is my home, everything that's important to me is here. I want to stay in Monks Quay always.'

'I could be happy here, too. Lancashire has good newspapers so I wouldn't need to go away to be a newspaperman. Nor would I,' Dan met and held her gaze as he raised the tankard to his lips, 'if I had reason enough to stay.'

'Isn't–' began Amy, breaking off as Fanny rustled towards them, still wearing her wedding dress.

'Do forgive me for interrupting you, Dan, but Theo and I are soon to leave.' She beamed down at them, her eyes sparkling mischievously. 'I need to steal Amy from you for just a little while – I'm sure she'll return directly!'

'What was all that about?' hissed Amy, when the sisters were indoors and on their way upstairs. 'You made it sound like–'

'Exactly!' Fanny swept into their room and whisked off her bonnet, sitting before the glass so Amy could fix her hair. 'Dan Ainsworth is smitten with you – that much is obvious! There's no need to be coy,' she went on, surveying her sister's flushed face in the mirror. 'The boy was sweet on you even at school – I clearly recall telling you so!'

'Fanny, for goodness sake!' Amy busied herself with the combs and pins. 'We were just children!'

'Well, he certainly isn't a child any longer!' Fanny arched an eyebrow, smoothing a ringlet around her finger. 'Nor are you. And you could do a lot worse than Dan Ainsworth. He's just about the only man in Monks Quay with an ounce of spark.'

'My wife and I are driving up to Whiteladies Grange to pay our respects to the Paslews,' Theodore was explaining to the gaggle of ladies clustered around him in the garden. 'My brother is staying on at Whiteladies for another month, while Fanny and I are travelling directly to Petherbridge for our honeymoon. Mr Paslew is very generously allowing us the use of his coach and driver for the journey – ah, here is my bride!' He beamed as Fanny emerged from the cottage in a becoming rose madder skirt and jacket. 'Am I not the most fortunate man alive, ladies?'

Fanny paused on the threshold, turning to give Amy a quick hug.

'If you hadn't stepped in to look after the family, I could never have married Theo,' she whispered, blinking back sudden tears. 'Thank you so much!'

'It's what I wanted,' mumbled Amy. 'Oh, Fan – I will miss you!'

'And I you – but York really isn't so far away. You must visit soon.'

But both sisters knew this would be their last meeting for a very long time.

'You mustn't worry about your new responsibilities,' continued Fanny softly. 'You'll manage splendidly. You're far more like Ma than I ever was.'

Then suddenly she was gone, out into the sunlit garden, with cheers and goodbyes ringing out around Clockmaker's Cottage as Theodore Buxton handed his new wife up into the Paslews' elegant open carriage with its tasteful festoons of satin ribbons, creamy-white hothouse blooms and glossy dark green foliage.

Holding her bridal posy in both hands,

Fanny closed her eyes tightly, but even so the flowers flew unerringly in Amy's direction.

Amy caught them tentatively, and another cheer went up as she buried her warm face in their sweet fragrance. Then another shower of rice and petals fluttered about the newly-weds as the gleaming bay mare shook her mane and moved sedately away upon the short journey to Whiteladies Grange.

'I'm glad you caught that bunch of flowers, lass.' Ramsay grinned. 'I thought that sister of yours was going to throw them at me! Now, where's Dan... Ah, Dan! We're setting up another round of horseshoes. Are you in?'

Dan Ainsworth gazed at Amy, standing a little away from everyone with the bridal flowers still in her arms. He drew breath to make comment, then thought better of it and turned toward Ramsay.

'You, me, Amos and Ned Yarkin, is it? Aye, count me in!'

Dusk was falling before the last of the merry-makers made their way home from Clock-maker's Cottage. Vicky was already fast asleep in her bed, worn out after the excite-ment of the day, and Amy, standing at the kitchen window washing the final few dishes, absently watched as Pa accompanied old Ned Yarkin as far as the garden gate.

The Mermaid's elderly potman had drunk and feasted well and was in fine fettle, doubtless setting the world to rights.

Suddenly though, Amy saw Pa wheel sharply to face Mr Yarkin, steadying the old man and addressing him intently. Ned Yarkin merely shook his head, clapped Ramsay on the shoulder a couple of times, bade his friend and neighbour goodnight and ambled on his way.

Seconds later, Ramsay MacFarlane thundered into the cottage, his weather-beaten features grim and his pale-blue eyes blazing.

'Where is he? Where's Rory?' he demanded of her. 'Ned Yarkin's just told me what happened in Monks Quay the other night! Why didn't *you* tell me, Amy? Were you hoping I'd not find out?'

'No!' she exclaimed in horror. 'No, Pa! It wasn't like–'

'You're in charge of this household now,' he went on angrily. 'I can't be here all the time, so I depend on you to take responsibility for what goes on while I'm away. I won't have Rory disgracing the family! Where is he–?'

'I'm here, Pa.' Rory stood in the doorway to the stairs, the smouldering rage in his eyes more than matching his father's. 'And I'm going out, so say your piece and I'll be on my way.'

'You'll not go anywhere till I get some answers, my lad!' Ramsay raised an accusing finger. 'You lied to me, Rory – and I can't abide a liar! A scrap with a bloke at the clay pits, was it? Summat and nowt, you said! Well, I'm waiting for the truth!'

Amy saw Rory's jaw tighten. His eyes narrowed, and the malicious glare he threw in her direction chilled her to the bone.

'What I do is my business.'

'No, it isn't – not while you're part of this family and living under my roof!' Ramsay banged the flat of his hand on the scrubbed table, surveying his son with disgust. 'What's up with you, Rory? Starting trouble at that thieves' den, The Green Man. Getting yourself senseless drunk and brawling in the street. Making a show of yourself in The Mermaid, gambling with men who could buy and sell you ten times over, and losing your wages! A whole week's wages on the turn of a card!'

Ramsay shook his head in disbelief.

'It's time you woke up to your respon-

65

sibilities to this family! You've a duty to pay your way. How do you think your sister is to manage with no money from you this week?'

'She'll just have to get used to it, won't she? Because I don't intend being around here much longer, anyhow!'

Striding past them both, Rory wrenched open the cottage door and stormed out through it, slammed it behind him.

The anger drained visibly from Ramsay's face, and Amy was shocked at how old and tired her father suddenly appeared.

'He lied to me, Amy,' he mumbled, without looking at her. 'The rest, I could've ... but my son lied to me.'

'I know, I know, Pa,' she murmured, already reaching for her shawl. 'I'm going after him.'

Amy had to run to catch up with Rory, snatching at his arm to halt him.

'Rory, I didn't–'

'Had to go running to Pa with tales about your big bad brother, didn't you?'

Shaking loose of her grasp, he rounded on her, gripping her narrow shoulders so fiercely she cried out.

'One word about them sovereigns and

you'll find out just how bad I can be!'

Shoving her roughly aside, he swiftly put distance between them.

Amy hesitated in the twilight, uncertain whether to return home, or to follow him and try to explain – and perhaps keep an eye on him, too, for such was his temper there was no guessing what he might do.

When, instead of taking the road into town, he cut across country towards White-ladies Grange, Amy's decision was made.

What purpose could he have for going to Whiteladies other than another clandestine meeting with Theodore Buxton before her brother-in-law and Fanny left for Pether-bridge?

She followed her brother warily, fearful lest he take a backward glance.

After a mile or so, he threw himself down on to the coarse grass next to the stone slab where, in olden days, on their way to the burial ground, the bearers would rest the coffins of the dead brought up from the sea.

Pressing into the shadows of the hedge-row, Amy waited. It was not long before a lone horseman cantered into sight along the track and her suspicions were confirmed.

Theodore didn't dismount, merely leaned down as her brother sprang to his feet and moved to the horse's side.

Few words were exchanged. Theodore handed a thick oblong package to Rory before sitting back in the saddle and gathering up the reins. He nodded, speaking as if issuing instructions and then, as Amy watched, he reached into his coat, withdrew a small object and passed this also to Rory.

Amy's breath, constricted in her chest, for in the pale glow of moonlight she clearly saw the gleaming barrel of a snub-nosed pistol resting in her wayward brother's hand.

Robbery!

'Try not to worry about her, Amy,' re-assured Anne Shawcross as they stood at the schoolhouse window watching Vicky, who was sitting cross-legged in the garden in the early morning sunshine.

With elbows planted on her knees, the little girl seemed mesmerised by the pollen-laden honey bees circling back and forth from their hives to the swatches of lavender, wild roses, clover and stock that were abundant in Anne's neat garden.

'It's true she's rather young to be joining school,' continued Anne, 'but she's very bright for her years.'

'I'd wanted to keep her at home until Pa sails, so she could share his last few days ashore,' said Amy. 'But he thought it better she start school straight away.'

'I'm in absolute agreement with your father, which doesn't occur very often,' replied Anne wryly. 'All Vicky has known until now is being at the cottage and having Fanny with her virtually every minute of every day. Now Fanny's married and gone, it's as well Vicky settles into the new routine before Ramsay leaves too.'

'I wish I could give up working at Whiteladies to stay at home to care for her and the rest of the family, as Fanny did.'

'Can you afford to?'

Amy shook her head. Despite Pa working hard all his life, first Ma and then Fanny had had to scrimp and save to make ends meet. And these past weeks, Rory had not given anything towards his keep.

He'd shrugged when Amy had tackled him about this. 'You know I lost all my brass, playing cards. How can I give you what I don't have?'

His sharp blue eyes had bored into hers, defying her to challenge him about that purse of sovereigns. But anxious not to stir up further trouble during Pa's short stay ashore, she'd held her tongue.

Now Amy met her aunt's gaze ruefully. 'We couldn't manage without my wages from Whiteladies. And I do enjoy working there, especially the sewing. Mrs Paslew's been ever so nice.'

'Eleanor Paslew's a good woman. Do your best for her, and you'll not go far wrong.' She paused, eyeing her favourite niece keenly. 'What's troubling you, child? I know your father and I don't get along and never shall, but I'm still family. I want to help, if I can. Is it Rory? Have he and your father fallen out?'

'Pa and Rory did have a set-to the night of the wedding,' answered Amy honestly. 'But if they've argued since, I haven't seen it.'

On the scant occasions she'd seen her father and brother together at Clockmaker's Cottage recently, there was stony silence between them and an atmosphere so tense it could be cut with a knife.

Rory was behaving as if nothing untoward had happened, and Amy couldn't help wondering if he was deliberately keeping out of Pa's way and biding his time until Ramsay sailed before carrying out whatever deed he and Theodore Buxton had been plotting that night they'd met at the resting place.

The burden of keeping silent about witnessing the exchange of package and pistol weighed heavily and constantly upon Amy. She longed for somebody to talk to, to confide in.

How she missed Fanny!

A keen easterly wind whipped ruddy colour

into Amy's cheeks as she hung out the laundry at Whiteladies Grange.

Propping the billowing lines high on the drying green, she stopped to pick up the baskets and hurried through the wash-house into the hot steamy kitchen.

'You'd best keep an eye out the window,' commented Gladys Braithwaite sagely. 'I feel rain in my bones. Now get them jars washed and dried, quick as you can – I can't trust Maisie to do it! If I've told that girl once that the jars have to be spotlessly clean and bone-dry else the preserves go mouldy, I've told her a hundred times but she still doesn't do the job right. Where is she, anyway?'

'Filling the scuttles, I think.'

The cook tutted in exasperation, tipping soft fruits and diced crab apples into one of the huge jamming pans.

'I sent her to fetch the coal half an hour since! She's as slow on the move as she is on the uptake! When you've a spare minute, I'll need more sugar grinding.'

Rolling up her sleeves, Amy drew the water and set it to boil before fetching the heavy wooden sugar box. Taking the hammer and flat blade, she cracked a generous slab from the sugar loaf and broke it into smaller pieces before dropping them a handful at a time into the grinder.

The basin of sparkling sugar granules was barely filled before the water bubbled to the boil and, hefting the tray of glass jars from the pantry's high shelf, she got started on sorting and washing.

The rain held off long enough for the day's laundry to be almost dry before Amy had to dart out and hastily take it down from the lines, bundling it into the baskets and racing back indoors.

'I know nowt about it, Gladys!' Dobson, the head gardener was just sitting himself down at the kitchen table. 'Mind, I've not been in the town this side of a fortnight.'

'Market day last week. That's when it happened. Edith Barraclough told me all about it when she brought over the butter and eggs this morning,' said Mrs Braithwaite, pouring her old friend a cup of tea. 'Left for dead, was what she said!'

'Who was he?'

'Nobody local. I think Edie said his name was Sydney Wallace or some such. Middle-aged, portly. Travelling salesman, she reckoned. Collie's cowman found him. Crawling up the lane towards the farmhouse. In a terrible state, he was! Blood–' she broke off, suddenly noticing Amy standing transfixed in the doorway from the wash-house. 'Don't just stand there gawping, girl! Get started preparing these vegetables Mr Dobson's brought, and sort the potatoes for roasting. You know by now the size I like them.'

Mrs Braithwhaite cast a long-suffering glance in the head gardener's direction, topping up his cup as she did so.

'Another slice of my date and walnut cake, Mr Dobson? Now, where was I? Oh, aye. This Mr Wallace had been set upon on the drovers' road toward Preston, just beyond The Green Man.'

'It's a rough house, is that.' Dobson chewed on his cake. 'Any one of them as drinks up at The Green Man is as likely to slit your throat as wish you time o' day. Gang of them set upon him, was there?'

'Nay, just the one! Mr Wallace was riding along and the villain came out of the dark at him. Dragged him to the ground, gave him a right thumping, stole his money and took his horse.'

'Horse thieving! You can hang for that!'

'That's another queer thing! The robber didn't keep the horse! Edie said, the day after poor Mr Wallace turned up at the farmhouse, one of the lads the Barracloughs have hired to lift their spuds spotted the horse wandering by the river!'

'So this Wallace feller got his horse back – I suppose that's summat.'

'No! No, he didn't, Mr Dobson! He'd already left Monks Quay on the first coach out! Didn't want to make a fuss, he said. Just wanted to get home to his wife and family. He even had to pawn his ring to pay for his coach fare,' reflected Mrs Braithwaite, crumbling a bit of fruit cake between her plump fingers. 'Collie Barraclough had seen Mr Wallace at The Mermaid on the night he got robbed. He'd had his dinner there and played a couple of hands of cards with Collie and the others. When word got round town about what had happened to him,' she concluded, 'Edie said Dan Ainsworth went looking all over for Mr Wallace.'

'What for? Why would young Dan be chasing this Wallace feller? He hadn't left The Mermaid without paying his bill, had he?'

'I don't know, do I? I only know what Collie told Edie,' replied Mrs Braithwaite impatiently. 'Besides, whatever Dan Ainsworth wanted with Mr Wallace, he was too late to get it – Wallace had already left on the first coach.'

'It's a rum do, is that,' considered Dobson, rubbing his stubbly chin. 'Fancy a thief not taking a good horse!'

'Whole thing's queer, if you ask me,' said Mrs Braithwaite, sniffily, stirring another spoonful of sugar into her tea. 'When Wallace was robbed, he was heading towards Preston. Yet the coach he took was going to Liverpool – it's as if he couldn't get away from Monks Quay quick enough, so had taken the first coach that was leaving the place, regardless of its destination!'

'I wouldn't want to hang round a place when I'd had the living daylights beaten out of me either,' muttered Dobson.

Amy's hands were deftly cleaning and preparing the vegetables for that evening's dinner, but inwardly she was reliving every moment of that awful morning when she and Dan had found Rory in Monks Quay.

Until now, she'd believed Rory had been brawling in the town that night. That had to be the reason for his cuts and bruises, surely? A middle-aged portly man on his way home to his family would not be capable of trading blows and inflicting such wounds upon a strong young man like Rory ... but where had the purse of sovereigns come from, if not from the pocket of the travelling salesman?

Surely her brother wasn't capable of attacking an innocent man and beating him to within an inch of his life? She couldn't – wouldn't – believe it, and yet … it all fitted. And what of Dan Ainsworth? Why had he wished to speak to this Mr Wallace? Dan had seen that purse of sovereigns every bit as clearly as she herself. Had he, too, put the pieces of the puzzle together?

Her suspicions wormed deeper and deeper as that endless day wore on. She was anxious to talk to Dan but Mrs Braithwaite had been in a crotchety mood all day long and Amy was convinced she'd be kept late at Whiteladies Grange that night.

'Amy! Amy! Have you got cloth ears or what?' The cook glared across the hot kitchen at her. 'The next batch is ready for bottling – it'll not jump into the jars by itself!'

With the huge jamming pan on the table between them, the two women were ladling scalding-hot strawberry preserve into warmed glass jars when the door from the passageway swung open and Miss Sophie strode into the kitchen.

'Excuse me, Mrs Braithwaite.' The Paslews's middle daughter beamed brightly. 'I need to borrow Amy.'

'She's not dressed for upstairs, miss.'

'I don't care about that.' Sophie turned her attention to Amy. 'Come along!'

'Beg pardon, Miss Sophie, but Amy has to stay here with me,' persisted Gladys Braithwaite. 'We're bottling, and it's not a job as can wait. It has to be done while the fruit is piping hot.'

'I'm sure anybody can do that with you, Mrs B,' returned Sophie pertly. 'I need Amy for something important!'

And the young woman turned on her heel.

Unsure whether to follow or stay put, Amy looked to Mrs Braithwaite.

The cook pursed her lips, and gave a quick nod of consent.

'Be as quick as you can. We've a lot to get done before we see our beds tonight!'

Wiping her hot, sticky hands on her apron as she went, Amy scurried after her young mistress and they reached the door into the main part of Whiteladies together. Amy hesitated.

'Miss Sophie, perhaps I'd better change my dress–'

'Stuff and nonsense! There's no time. This is an absolute emergency!'

Swinging open the heavy oak door, she swept up the wide staircase and along the landing to her room.

'Sit down, Amy, and I'll tell you all about it!'

'I don't think I'd better, miss,' protested Amy quietly.

She was hot and dishevelled. Wisps of damp hair clung to her neck and her temples, and her cheeks were red and shiny from the kitchen's heat.

'I'm not allowed up here in my kitchen clothes, and anyway I'm sticky from the jam-making.'

'Ah! Yes, I see what you mean,' conceded Sophie. 'Very well, go and tidy yourself – but don't dawdle.'

After hurriedly washing her face, combing her hair and changing into her upstairs clothes, Amy returned to find Sophie staring disconsolately at an assortment of dresses, skirts and bodices strewn across her bed.

'I just don't have a single thing suitable!' she exclaimed without turning around. 'I'd really like to wear this new skirt, but all of the bodices look so dreary with it. What do you think?'

Amy considered the skirt with its cream

and brown woven stripes radiating from the broad waistband, and the array of bodices tossed higgledy-piggledy all around it.

'This high-necked one with the full sleeves would look well with the skirt, and the buttermilky colour matches the brown and cream nicely.'

'Yes, but it'll be a fearfully dull outfit and this is such a special occasion,' responded Sophie plaintively. 'Clemmie and I have been invited by Amelia Deane and her brother, Laurence, to a garden party at Rufford. Amelia always dresses exquisitely – the absolute height of fashion – and although she's the most awful person, I just have to be at that garden party! You see, I really do like Laurence Deane and I'm desperate to make an impression upon him. I was telling Clemmie how unbearably dreary all my clothes are,' went on Sophie. 'And she said perhaps you could embellish them with your beautiful embroidery. You could, couldn't you? Oh, do say you can, Amy! I can't bear to look drab and sensible at the garden party, I want Laurence to find me pretty and utterly captivating!'

Amy chewed her lip, smoothing her fingertips over the delicate fabric of the buttermilk bodice. She sewed well, but she'd never attempted anything so ambitious. One mistake, and the lovely garment would be ruined.

'I could embroider a floral spray on the left side, perhaps. With some fine beading – there are some beautiful little crystal beads in the sewing-box – and the floral pattern could be repeated in tiny garlands upon the cuffs and high collar.' Amy raised her eyes hesitantly to Sophie's eager face. 'If you think that might be suitable, miss?'

'Perfect! I can see it already! Could you make some matching flowers to trim my bonnet?'

'I've never made flowers, miss!'

'Oh, I'm sure you'll manage wonderfully. The garden party's only a few days away, so you must begin straight away–' she paused at a quiet tapping upon her door. 'Come!'

'Sophie, are you–' Gilbert Paslew stood on the threshold, breaking off as his astonished gaze swept the room. 'Has a whirlwind passed this way, or did you simply decide to throw your clothes about for the sheer exhilaration of it?'

'I didn't have anything to wear for the garden party,' she replied. 'Amy's come to my rescue! She's going to make me look so beautiful; Laurence Deane will find me utterly irresistible!'

'Got a magic wand, has she?' His gaze slid in Amy's direction, and she saw his grey eyes were twinkling. 'And a large book of spells?'

'Beast!' Sophie bundled up a mauve jacket and hurled it at her older brother. 'It's terribly important that everything goes perfectly. I intend inviting the Deans to Whiteladies during the summer, and since it's Amelia who decides which invitations they accept, I'm relying on you to win her over. It's up to you to ensure Amelia can't wait to visit us at Whiteladies!'

'Why me? Why can't Nicholas win her over?'

'Because Nick will be accompanying Clemmie and, besides, you're my brother! You're supposed to help me. This garden party is my first opportunity to get to know Laurence properly, and I need you to spirit Amelia away and to keep her occupied for the afternoon.'

'In order that you may use your wiles on her brother?'

'Yes. I do so like him, Gilbert, but you know how quiet and shy he is!'

'He's probably not quiet at all,' returned Gilbert, leaning a shoulder against the door jamb. 'The poor blighter just never gets the chance to open his mouth with a sister like Amelia.'

'All the more reason for you to help me!' she implored. 'Sweep her off her feet. Use your charm for goodness sake!'

'I doubt charm will be effective where Amelia Deane is concerned,' commented Gilbert sceptically, catching Amy's eye once more. 'A scold's bridle is more suited to the task.'

Amy was following the discourse with increasing agitation. She could not leave the room without being dismissed, yet time was racing away and with every passing minute Mrs Braithwaite would become more and more vexed by her absence.

'Don't be mean—'

'I'll do my best,' he interrupted quietly. 'Laurence is a decent chap and he deserves to meet a nice, gentle girl – meanwhile, I daresay he'll have to make do with you. Now don't you think you've taken up enough of Amy's valuable time?'

'What?' Sophie turned to Amy, her face blank. 'Oh, I'd quite forgotten you were still here. Yes, you may go back to the kitchen, but put away these clothes first.' She strode to the door, following her brother on to the landing. 'Remember,' she called over her shoulder, 'I must have the bodice and flowers before Friday!'

Their voices disappeared down the staircase and Amy began gathering up the strewn clothes. Most would need a good pressing before they were returned to the wardrobes. There were hours of extra work here! With sinking spirits, she raced down the backstairs to face the sharp edge of Mrs Braithwaite's tongue.

It was indeed very late when Amy finally hung up her apron at Whiteladies Grange and sped through Friars Wood into the lane that led towards the schoolhouse. She wasn't surprised to find the small dwelling completely in darkness, nor to read the note pinned upon the low door.

When Amy hadn't returned from Whiteladies by the given hour, Aunt Anne had taken Vicky home. She would also have prepared supper for the family at Clockmaker's Cottage and put Vicky to bed, if necessary.

Amy sighed with weariness and gratitude. It had been a long, fraught day, and exhaustion suddenly got the better of her. Sinking on to the cold stone doorstep of the schoolhouse, she rested her head in her hands. All she wanted was to get home and fall into her bed but she really did need to speak to Dan Ainsworth without delay.

Getting to her feet once more, she set off towards the town and The Mermaid Inn. Hurrying through the archway into the stable yard, she tapped at the side door and waited patiently. When Ned Yarkin finally opened up, she was greatly relieved to see a familiar face.

'Good evening, Mr Yarkin. Could – could I see Dan, please?'

'You're out late, lass.' The elderly potman smiled at her. 'I'll fetch him out for you.'

His footsteps shuffled away, and presently Dan emerged from the dark passageway.

'This is a nice surprise.'

'Can I ask you about something, Dan?'

''Course. Come in–'

'It's … private.'

'Stables then.' He reached for her arm and started across the shadowy yard. 'The cobbles are uneven, so mind your step. Here we are.'

Closing the large doors behind them, Dan led the way inside. Lighting a lantern and hanging it upon a harness hook, he indicated a straw bale to Amy and sat himself on the rungs of the loft ladder.

'Is it all right if the horses hear whatever

you have to say?'

She smiled in spite of her fatigue. Several of the horses were peering around from their stalls to consider her with large, shining, brown eyes.

'Mrs Braithwaite and Mr Dobson were talking today about a man who was attacked and robbed last market night,' she began, facing Dan in the flickering lantern light and somehow already beginning to feel better. 'She said you'd wanted to talk to him, but he'd already left on the coach.'

'Yes, well – he'd pawned his ring to pay the fare. It struck me as odd the thief didn't take Wallace's ring – and his horse – as well as his money. Both would be worth a fair bit,' commented Dan reflectively. 'Mind, there's quite a few things don't square up right. Wallace knew I was looking for him, and I had the notion he kept giving me the slip because he didn't want to talk too much about what had happened that night. He boarded that coach quick as snap, and I lost my chance. Pity, too. It would've made a grand story.'

Amy shook her head, not understanding. 'What do you mean?'

'It's the closest thing to proper news we've had in Monks Quay for a fair while and the mystery about the ring and the horse not being taken make it all the more interesting,' responded Dan. 'I wrote to the editor of *The Lancashire Clarion* months ago, and he said if I sent in a report of local news he'd gladly read it. But Sydney Wallace left for Liverpool before I could pin him down and get some proper details.'

'You were going to write about this in a newspaper?' She stared at him, aghast.

'Amy, I want to be a newspaperman!' he exclaimed. '*The Clarion* might not be *The Guardian* or *The Times*, but it would've been a start!'

'It's wrong, Dan!' she cried emotionally. 'To even think about telling the whole of Lancashire about this–'

'Because Rory might be the robber?' he cut in. 'That's what you're thinking, isn't it? That Rory did it, and if I'd written about it in *The Clarion*, that other folk besides you and me might start thinking the same?'

'No! Rory wouldn't–' but the denial died on her lips.

'Wouldn't he?' demanded Dan harshly. 'I know what I think.'

Amy clasped her hands tightly in her lap, unable to raise her eyes and meet his clear gaze as the silence lengthened between them.

'What *do* you think?' she mumbled at last. 'Because I don't know what to believe any more. Pa heard Rory was brawling in town that night. And we did find him the next morning, didn't we?'

'Huh! Rory was up to a sight more that night than scrapping!' returned Dan briskly. 'Sydney Wallace was in The Mermaid early the previous evening. He had his meal and played some cards. Then I saw him and Theodore Buxton sitting in the back room with their heads together, and Buxton wasn't looking any too pleased. I don't know when Wallace left, but after Rory came in and lost all his money, him and Buxton were in a huddle over a couple of tots of rum. Then Rory was gone, and a few hours later Wallace was attacked on the drovers' road.'

Amy ran her tongue over dry lips. Theodore Buxton again!

'I've poked around town. Asked a few questions. I've no proof what happened. It's just my opinion.'

She swallowed hard, her heart hammering.

'Tell me what you think happened.'

'I reckon there were dealings between Buxton and Sydney Wallace, but it turned sour and Buxton sent Rory after him,' said

88

Dan evenly. 'Wallace wasn't fit enough or young enough to put up a fight. Rory stole his money right enough, but left the ring and probably rode the horse back to The Green Man before turning it loose. He had a few more drinks, ended up in Tanners Row and the rest we know.'

'I can't believe you were going to print all this in a newspaper just to – to feed your ambitions!' She rose unsteadily, her eyes sparkling. 'It's despicable, Dan. How could you? How could you!'

Crossing the stable in a couple of strides, Dan was before her as she turned to leave.

'Ask yourself a question, Amy. Why are you so angry? Then face up to the answer – because, like me, you believe it was your brother who robbed Sydney Wallace and left him for dead on the drovers' road!'

Rory Leaves Home

The bells of All Hallows were ringing out as the MacFarlanes walked across the meadow to services that Sunday morning.

'If I was ashore all the while, I'd like to ring the bells,' remarked Ramsay, helping Vicky clamber over the stile. 'I always fancied myself as a bell-ringer. My father rang the bells in the pit town where he was born, just as his father did before him. Then when Father left Scotland for the mines in the Isle of Man, he rang at his local kirk. I had a go myself as a lad in Laxey.'

'Perhaps I'd better take it up,' suggested Edmund with a smile. 'And keep it in the family!'

'If bell-ringing's to be kept in this family, then it'll certainly have to be you who does it! I somehow can't see Rory taking it up – we were lucky he came to church for his sister's wedding! Though to be fair to the lad,' Ramsay went on seriously, 'he's shaped up a fair bit since I came ashore. Hasn't stayed out late or gone drinking up at The

Green Man, lately. All credit to him if he's mended his ways and is working hard, because he's got the ability to do a lot better for himself than Paslew's clay pits!'

Amy's heart ached at meeting Pa's earnest eyes, understanding how deeply he wanted to believe the best and to be proud of his eldest son.

Vicky was skipping ahead of them, and Edmund was talking to Pa about helping lift potatoes at Barraclough's farm ready for when the Jenet Rae set sail, but Amy was so wrapped up in her own sombre thoughts, that she scarcely heard a word.

When they reached All Hallows, Edmund strode across to meet Nicholas Buxton, who had just arrived in the Paslews' carriage, and the rest of the MacFarlane family went on, and into the church.

Taking her place in the choir stalls, Amy watched absently as Pa and Vicky settled into their usual pew. Vicky had spotted one of her new school friends, and waved wildly to the red-haired little girl in a gingham pinafore. She'd taken to school like a duck to water, and it was lovely to see her so happy and excited.

Amy breathed in the calming atmosphere of the Norman church. Her aunt Anne nodded in her direction as she passed by, speaking quietly with Reverend Linley as she sat at the organ and unfolded her music. Not many folk in Monks Quay could play the organ, and those who could took turns at playing for services.

The church was filling as the congregation gradually filed in. Among the last to enter were the Paslews. Mr and Mrs Paslew and their daughters made their way to the family pew near the lady chapel, and Amy caught herself wondering if Miss Sophie had been pleased with the buttermilk bodice and bonnet flowers she'd spent so many painstaking hours making.

After studying the Paslew sisters for a minute or two, Amy decided Sophie looked particularly animated, so perhaps the outfit, the garden party, and the bid to impress her young man had been successful!

Her gaze drifted once more to the west door, where the final few parishioners were hurrying inside.

Gilbert Paslew, Nicholas Buxton and Edmund were bringing up the rear, exchanging a final few words before going their separate ways.

With a pang, Amy realised she was looking out for Dan Ainsworth. His parents and younger brothers were seated a few rows behind the MacFarlanes, but Dan was not with them. Amy chided herself for feeling so very disappointed not to see him, for he rarely came to church except at Christmas and suchlike.

She scarcely noticed Gilbert Paslew slipping unobtrusively into the back row of the choir stalls before the music swelled beneath Aunt Anne's deft fingertips, and then Reverend Linley stepped up into the pulpit and All Hallows' Sunday Service commenced.

'You all go on ahead, I want to catch up with Harry Smedley,' her father was saying as they left the church, nodding to where the miller and his family were climbing up on to their cart. 'I'll see you back at Clockmaker's.'

'Very well, Pa.' Amy paused, waiting for Edmund to join them. He was once more deep in conversation with Nicholas Buxton and Gilbert Paslew.

'Edmund's become very friendly with Nicholas, hasn't he?' observed Anne. 'I must say, he seems a thoroughly nice, considerate person. Quite a different character from his elder–' She broke off as the three young men came within earshot.

'Aunt Anne! Gilbert's offered to give me

some of his books for my scholarship work!' began Edmund enthusiastically, as he joined the rest of his family. 'He has all the Greek ones you said I should study!'

'That's thoughtful of you, Gilbert.' Anne nodded approval. 'It will be of enormous help for Edmund to have access to those texts.'

'Books should be read and used and discussed, Miss Shawcross – you taught me that a long time ago. It's very rewarding to pass them on to somebody like Edmund, who's really interested in all they have to say.'

'My nephew has a sharp intellect and we have great hopes for his future,' she replied, adding, 'I was pleased to hear you singing in the choir again, Gilbert. We need a good strong tenor. May I assume you're intending to stay at Monks Quay?'

'Yes. Uncle William – the Reverend Linley – and I have been talking at length this summer about the choir, and a great deal more besides. You see, during my last year at Oxford I was seriously considering the priesthood. However, I'm still not certain that I have a true vocation,' replied Gilbert, adding drily. 'Of course, my father is delighted I've finally seen sense and am returning to Monks Quay to join the family business!'

'Hardly surprising,' commented Anne crisply. 'You are his only son and heir! May I add your name to the organ-playing rota?'

'Please do! Although I'm frightfully rusty and will need hours of practice before I'm fit for the ears of the congregation.' He made to take his leave, pausing to smile at Amy. 'I understand you were responsible for gathering and arranging the flowers this week, Miss MacFarlane? The church looked especially beautiful today.'

'Thank you,' Amy murmured, warm colour rising to her cheeks as Gilbert Paslew held her gaze.

Then the moment was broken and, raising his hat and bidding them all a friendly good day, he strode across the churchyard towards the bridle path that lead to Whiteladies Grange.

'I won't be in for dinner, Amy. Nicholas and I are borrowing Dan Ainsworth's boat and sailing out to Fiddler's Pike and back this afternoon,' announced Edmund.

'Dan?' echoed Amy blankly. 'You've seen Dan?'

'Of course! Since I've been lifting potatoes out at Barraclough's farm, I see Dan all the time when I'm going through town.'

Edmund gave a cheery wave as he and Nicholas headed off up the coast to the boathouses. 'See you later!'

'Enjoy yourselves!' she called after them. 'Be careful – mind the sandbanks and keep well clear of Judas Rocks!'

With Vicky running on ahead, Amy fell into step beside Aunt Anne as they strolled across the meadows away from All Hallows.

She hadn't seen Dan since that night in the stables, yet he'd scarcely been absent from her thoughts. After their quarrel, she no longer felt able to go to The Mermaid Inn simply to chat to him. If only it were possible for her to bump into him as casually and often as Edmund evidently did!

Aunt Anne's voice jarred her from her reverie.

'I wonder what your father wanted with Harry Smedley?' pondered Anne, tightening the ribbons of her bonnet against the freshening breeze as the sea and Clockmaker's Cottage came into view. 'Ah, well, I daresay we'll find out in due course!'

Rory had still been asleep when the family had left for church. Now, upon their return, he was nowhere to be found.

With the dinner cooking nicely, and Aunt Anne and Vicky out gathering gooseberries for the rice pudding they'd have at tea time before Pa sailed – and Pa himself not yet back from his talk with Harry Smedley – Amy went upstairs to tidy her brothers' room and to make their beds.

Gathering together the dirty washing, she emptied their pockets before taking the garments down to the tub, and almost cried out when, turning from the task, she found Rory standing behind her.

'Well, well, little sister! Looking for something?'

She faced him squarely and in that instant was utterly convinced that proof or no proof, Dan Ainsworth had been right.

'If you're looking for a purse of sovereigns to give back to their proper owner,' he sneered, 'you'll not find 'em here!'

'It was you, wasn't it?' she asked, her gaze steady. 'You attacked and robbed Sydney Wallace.'

'Sydney Wallace?' echoed Rory wryly. 'Who's he when he's at home?'

'Could you really have wanted that money so badly you'd do something so wicked?'

'Wallace was working for a friend of mine, but he got greedy and started taking a slice

97

of the profits. I did this friend a favour by teaching Wallace a lesson – and made myself a pretty penny or two into the bargain!'

'You're in league with Theodore Buxton!'

'Is that a fact?' he taunted. 'Well, I'm not fretting you'll shop me. Nor will Dan Ainsworth. He could, but he won't. Because of you. Poor beggar's smitten!'

'It's not too late to mend your ways,' she implored. 'You can never put right what you did to Sydney Wallace, but you don't have to continue with whatever wickedness you and Theodore Buxton are plotting! It'll break Pa's heart if he ever learns the truth. You must stop, Rory. Stop now, please!'

'Stop! Stop?' he mocked, watching her horrified expression as he slid the pistol from the pocket of his coat, extending his palm so she might see it more closely. 'Why, me and this little beauty haven't even started yet!'

Amy could only stare at the deadly weapon as both she and her brother stood perfectly motionless. The rattle of the front gate finally broke the heavy silence, and Rory returned the pistol to his pocket.

'Do I hear the family returning?' He arched an eyebrow, stepping aside so Amy might quit the room ahead of him. 'Let's go down and eat dinner, shall we?'

Amy didn't taste a mouthful of the delicious meal she'd cooked for the family, nor hear a word of the conversation, despite this being Pa's last few hours at home before he sailed with the potato crop to the Isle of Man.

As soon as she and Aunt Anne started clearing the table, Rory scraped back his chair.

'Before you go dashing off, son, I want to talk to you,' said Ramsay.

'I've things to do.'

'I daresay, but this'll not take long. Sit down, lad. It's important.'

Shrugging, Rory sat and folded his arms.

Amy and her aunt exchanged glances.

Setting down a pile of crockery upon the board, Anne crossed to the step where Vicky was playing with her rag doll.

'Shall we collect some gooseberries for tea?'

'But we've already picked lots of berries today!'

'You can never have too many gooseberries with a rice pudding,' replied Anne, firmly ushering the child outdoors. 'That's what I always say...'

'Son, I've had a talk with Harry Smedley,'

began Ramsay, and Amy could hear the pride in her father's quiet voice and see the light in his eyes as he looked across the table at his eldest son. 'His mill's prospering – the packet's carrying more and more of Smedley's flour with every year that goes by – and since Harry needs another strong lad up at the mill, he's willing to take you on. You start tomorrow morning and–'

'Hang on, I've had enough of this!' cut in Rory, shaking his head in disbelief. 'You went cap in hand to Harry Smedley and got me a job without a word to me? Smedley knows what he can do with his milling, for I want no part of it!'

'Rory! I only want what's best for you, son!' persisted Ramsay earnestly. 'You'll be set for life once you've a proper trade to your name. You can maybe go into business yourself one day. It's a grand opportunity!'

'When will you realise, Pa? I'm done bowing and scraping to the likes of Paslew and Harry Smedley,' declared Rory, snatching his coat from the chair back. 'I've got plans – plans as'll take me far away from Monks Quay. I'm off into town. I'll not see you again before you sail with the tide.'

Pulling on his coat, Rory paused at the threshold. His anger and resentment seemed

100

suddenly to subside and he briefly met Ramsay's gaze before turning away.

'Have a safe trip, Pa.'

Standing at the quayside that evening, Amy longed to comfort her father before he sailed. However, she no more had the words to do so now than when Rory had gone from Clockmaker's and left her and Pa alone in the quiet cottage.

'Do you have to go away?' Vicky was saying, clutching Ramsay's callused hand tightly. 'I don't want you to go!'

'I don't want to go, either.' He laughed, swinging her up into his arms. As he hugged the little girl, Amy noticed his gaze travelling along the quayside and up towards the town. Poor Pa! He was still hoping Rory would relent and come to bid him farewell.

'Edmund, you've grown up all of a sudden and I'm right proud of you!' said Ramsay thickly, putting down Vicky and then impulsively wrapping his arms about the boy's narrow shoulders. 'You did a man's job lifting those spuds for Barraclough – the Jenet Rae couldn't have sailed without 'em!'

Turning to Amy, he smiled down at her. 'You're your ma's daughter and no mistake!

Take care of your brothers and sister for me, lass.'

'I will, Pa! Don't worry – about anything. Just come home safe!'

A final wave from the deck, and the Jenet Rae, laden with her cargo of potatoes and grain and riding low in the water, set sail and was borne away on the tide. A lump leapt to Amy's throat. Pa was gone, and she'd never felt so alone before.

When Amy came down from putting Vicky to bed that night, Edmund glanced up from his reading. It was the first opportunity they'd had to talk.

'Did Pa and Rory have another row today?'

'Yes. Why do you ask?'

'I think he's gone.'

Alarm – and fear – gripped her.

'Whatever do you mean?'

'I may be mistaken,' he went on hastily. 'But when I was in our room earlier, I noticed that although his work clothes and boots are still there, his razor and other bits and pieces weren't on his shelf.'

'Rory said he had plans!' Expelling a slow breath, Amy sat down at the table. 'But to just up and go without a word...'

'We'll manage without him,' responded Edmund firmly. 'You, Vicky and me. Don't worry, Amy. It'll be all right, you'll see!'

Presently, she left Edmund to his studies and stepped out into the gathering dusk. Ragged clouds were drifting across the night sky and she walked briskly along the hard, damp sand towards one of her favourite haunts.

Clambering up on to the smooth, time-worn hogsback rock, she sat and stared far away into the blackness of the distant sea. Pa and the Jenet Rae were out there some-where. He and his crew had worked hard to make good what repairs they could, but what if their efforts were not enough...? She was overwhelmed with foreboding. What if the packet got into difficulties, as Pa said she might? Suppose – Amy squeezed her eyes tightly shut.

'Amy!' The low voice came to her from the dark. 'It's only me!'

'Dan!' she gasped, tearful at the sudden happiness of seeing him.

'I knocked at Clockmaker's, and when Edmund said you'd gone for a walk, I thought I might find you here.'

'I'm so glad to see you, Dan! And I'm sorry for making such a fuss about the newspaper story.'

'I spoke out of turn myself that night!' He smiled, sitting down beside her. 'Did your da get away all right?'

She nodded, her gaze once more drawn out to the vast emptiness of the sea.

Suddenly, she could keep her silence no longer. She had to tell someone, and Dan was the only person in whom she could confide.

'Rory's gone, Dan! Gone for good, I think. He did attack Mr Wallace on the drovers' road...' And out poured the whole story – the clandestine meetings she'd witnessed at both All Hallows and the resting place; the package, the pistol – everything.

'You shouldn't have kept this to yourself,' he murmured when she'd finished. 'You can tell me anything. You know that.'

'I know,' she mumbled. Unexpected emotion was welling deep within her and she looked away from him quickly, sudden tears stinging her eyes.

'There, there, lass,' he comforted, tentatively reaching an arm about her trembling shoulders. Gently drawing her closer, he rested his cheek against the softness of her hair. 'I'm here for you, Amy. And here I'll be for as long as ever you want me...'

An Adventure For Amy

Although what little breeze there was, blew away from Amy as she stood beating carpets on the drying green at Whiteladies Grange, she felt grimy and covered in dust from head to toe.

Her raised arms were aching from hours of wielding the large wooden beater, but even so, her thoughts were far removed from the chore of cleaning the drawing-room carpets.

In her mind's eye, she was re-reading Fanny's latest letter which had arrived earlier that day with the coach from York.

'*The months are passing so swiftly,*' Fanny had written in her beautiful, formal hand, '*it already seems a lifetime ago since I was with you all at Clockmaker's Cottage. Our honeymoon trip to Petherbridge is now but a distant memory and we are thoroughly installed here in our home at Carteret Square.*

While the house is not perhaps as large as I had imagined it, it is beautifully proportioned with spacious rooms, splendid high ceilings and the most impressive fireplaces! Oh, I do wish you could see it all, Amy! Every room is furnished so tastefully, and everything is so fine and comfortable. My new home is even more than I ever dreamed a house could be!

We haven't yet entertained; however, I am planning my first ever dinner party! I am at once excited and apprehensive! From working at Whiteladies Grange you have some notion of the ways of people of quality. I have no such experience and am anxious about making mistakes and disappointing and embarrassing Theo.

I shall have a new gown for the dinner party. Theo insists upon it. He is the most dear and generous husband imaginable. I scarcely would have thought it possible to be so happy, and I hope you marry as well and wisely as I have! How is Dan Ainsworth by the way...?'

Amy could picture her sister's arch smile as she wrote those words!

'Carteret Square is within sight of the Minster and, when Theo is away from home on matters of business, it is a very pleasant stroll for me to attend evensong; Theo, alas, is not a churchgoer, so we don't attend services together. Now we are firmly established in York, he is always so very busy and I fear his absences upon business will become more frequent. After the bustle of Clockmaker's Cottage, I confess to feeling very alone in this big house whenever he is gone. I'll welcome

Nicholas's company when he returns from Whiteladies. I don't suppose he'll accompany Theo on business trips. I can't envisage Nicholas as a shrewd man of commerce, can you?

Last week, Theo and I went to the ballet, and a few evenings before that to a production of Hamlet. Wherever we go, we seem to bump into all manner of wealthy, important people and my husband knows them all. I'm so very proud to be his wife, and I still can't quite believe he chose me when he might so easily have wed the daughter of an influential family here in York.

This really is the most lively and fascinating place, Amy! Everyday on my walks and drives I discover new sources of interest. Oh, I meant to tell you something in my last letter and quite forgot. I thought I saw Rory, here in York!

Theo and I had arranged to meet for luncheon, but I was rather early so was browsing along Petergate. I'd stopped to look in the windows of a draper there, when a man came out from the coffee house across the street – I particularly noticed because it was one of the coffee houses Theo frequents. At first glance I thought it was Rory, but he strode away so quickly I wasn't able to get a really good look at him. And besides, although the man I saw wasn't a gentleman, he appeared well-groomed and smartly dressed – quite unlike our brother!'

Finally finishing the carpet-beating, Amy dusted down her apron with her hands before starting indoors. There was no doubt in her mind that it had been Rory who Fanny had seen in York. Putting two and two together, wasn't it likely he'd been at the coffee house to meet Theodore Buxton and to discuss whatever dealings the pair had together? Dealings that were apparently bringing prosperity to Rory...

Replacing the carpet beater in its cupboard, she hurried along the passageway past the kitchen where Mrs Braithwaite was sharing a pot of tea with Edith Barraclough, who made use of her regular trips up to Whiteladies with eggs, butter and milk to have a sup and chat with her old friend.

'Amy!' called Edie Barraclough, glimpsing her from the corner of her eye as she passed the open doorway. 'If your Edmund wants more work up at the farm will you tell him Collie says he has only to knock on the door and ask? There's usually summat for a hardworking lad to do around the place.'

'Thanks, Mrs Barraclough, but Edmund really needs to concentrate on his studies from now on. I don't want him working regularly.'

'Don't dally over getting yourself cleaned

up and presentable, girl,' commented Gladys Braithwaite sharply. 'There's fresh flowers needed upstairs!'

Washed and wearing her black dress and a clean apron, Amy took the trug and followed the paths that meandered through the flower gardens.

While selecting blooms suitable for the ladies' posy bowls and the crystal vases in the dining and drawing-rooms, she could hear the murmur of voices from the south-facing terrace and could see that Alfred and Gilbert Paslew were taking their coffee there, apparently discussing the documents that Alfred Paslew had spread out on the table before them.

An hour or so later, Amy was in the drawing-room, arranging the flowers, when Alfred Paslew strode in, with his two younger daughters following.

'Absolutely not, Sophie!' He noticed Amy, who immediately bobbed a curtsey and made to quit the room. 'Stay where you are, girl. Carry on with what you're doing – Sophie, I refuse to squander money on constructing an orangery just so that you can impress your young man!'

'Laurence isn't my young man,' she protested, adding coyly. 'Not yet.'

'I'm sure he will be if that's what you've decided upon,' commented Paslew, crossing to the writing desk and taking an inventory from the blotter.

'Please, Father!' persisted Sophie. 'An orangery would be so ... exquisite!'

'Exquisite and expensive, although not necessarily in that order,' he retorted, running a shrew eye down the list in his hands. 'I'm perfectly happy for you to have your parties and whatever else, providing I don't need to do more than greet your guests and be passably civil to them. Anything more is quite out of the question.'

'Very well, Father,' replied Sophie meekly, elbowing her younger sister sharply in the ribs.

'Might we have new dresses, then?' piped up Clemmie dutifully. 'Particularly Sophie. It'd be dreadful if she was shown up by Laurence's sister!'

'Amelia has such ... flair!' chipped in Sophie.

'Amelia Deane has a father with more money than sense,' said Paslew, consulting his pocket watch with a frown. 'Ah, there you are, Gilbert! Ready to go? Good! I have the inventory, and you've amended the contract, haven't you?'

'Father!' Sophie pursued him from the drawing-room into the hall. 'May Clemmie and I go to Liverpool, just to buy a very few things?'

'You'll have to see your mother about that.'

Taking his hat, Alfred Paslew strode to the front door.

Gilbert Paslew paused in the drawing-room, smiling across at Amy. 'More beautifully arranged flowers, Miss MacFarlane – they really are lovely!'

But before Amy could return his smile, Gilbert had followed his father through the hall and out to the waiting horses.

She watched from the window as father and son cantered down the drive and took the northbound ride beyond the gates of Whiteladies Grange.

'Erm … Amy.'

She spun around to find Clemmie Paslew hovering behind her, and at once bobbed a curtsey.

'I – I'd like you to accept this.' Clemmie stepped forward, stretching out her hand and offering Amy a neatly-wrapped little package. 'It's, well, it's my way of thanking you for the runner. It was the nicest surprise. That corner of the garden is my special place, you see. And you depicted it beautifully.'

'Thank you, miss,' murmured Amy, quite taken aback.

She glanced across at the other girl, guessing they were about the same age.

Clemmie Paslew was plump, rather plain, and seemed very shy and unsure.

'I love flowers and plants,' explained Amy, 'and I love sewing too, so...'

Her voice trailed off awkwardly, and both girls suddenly smiled at each other, their difference in station momentarily forgotten.

'I've wanted to give you a present for ages!' exclaimed Clemmie. 'But I didn't have anything I thought you'd like. When I heard Gilbert was going to Liverpool on business for Father, I asked him to get these from Mosleys' – the haberdasher's in Bold Street – I do hope you like them!'

The little parcel had burned a hole in Amy's apron pocket all day long. However, with Mrs Braithwaite's eagle eye upon her she hadn't had the opportunity to open it up.

'You'll never guess what happened today at Whiteladies!' she began telling Dan when he met her at the schoolhouse that evening.

'Paslew promised to pay you a decent

wage and to give you a day off every week?'

'Better than that!' returned Amy blithely, beaming up at him.

Dan had taken to meeting her every evening when she went to collect Vicky from Aunt Anne's.

'Miss Clemmie gave me a thank-you gift because she was so pleased with some needlework I did for her.'

She dipped her hand into her pocket and took out the little package. Slowly, she untied the string and unfolded the paper, lifting the lid of a small, square box.

'Oh, Dan! Look! Aren't they beautiful?'

He looked down over her shoulder. 'It's a pair of scissors.'

'Proper sewing scissors!' exclaimed Amy, carefully taking the finely-crafted swan-necked silver scissors in her hand.

'What a thoughtful gift!'

'It's not hard to be thoughtful when you've got money.'

'Ohhhh … you!' She laughed, shaking her head as they followed Vicky across the meadows towards Clockmaker's Cottage.

'We had another letter from Fanny this morning,' she went on. 'She's very happy and loves living in York, but she thought she saw Rory coming from a coffee house near the Minster. Do you think it was him, Dan? Fanny couldn't be certain.'

'Likely as not it was,' he told her, his hand upon the cottage gate. 'I wonder what he and Theodore Buxton are up to? Nothing on the right side of the law, that's for sure!'

'Are you coming in for a cup of tea?' she asked, suddenly loath to see him go. 'Perhaps you could stay for supper?'

'Thank you, but I've got to get back to The Mermaid. The coach from Preston will be arriving within the hour.' He paused, holding her gaze for a long moment. 'I'd best be on my way... See you tomorrow.'

She nodded, watching him start back towards town, then turned with a sigh and went indoors.

The meal was over and cleared. Vicky was in bed, and Amy was replacing the buttons on Edmund's school shirt, her silver swan-necked scissors on the table beside her. Despite Dan's scornfulness, she felt a glow of happiness whenever her gaze rested upon them.

The evening was drawing on towards dusk when the cottage gate creaked and the door knocker was hesitantly rattled.

'Good evening, Miss MacFarlane.'

'Mr Paslew!'

'Gilbert, please! Is Edmund at home? I promised I'd dig out some books about the Greek victory at Marathon–' His face broke into a broad smile and he indicated the weighty tomes in his arms. 'As you can see, I've done just that!'

'Edmund's outside, chopping wood.' She smiled, stepping aside in welcome. 'Won't you come in?'

Showing Gilbert to a seat, she hastily cleared her sewing from the table and he noticed her scissors. 'I see Clemmie gave you her present!'

'They're beautiful!' she responded. 'I understand you chose them. Thank you.'

'I was merely the errand boy following strict instructions! Clemmie was touched at the care behind the runner you made for her,' Gilbert went on seriously. 'Although she doesn't say much, Clemmie does feel things deeply – unlike Sophie!' His grey eyes were suddenly mischievous. 'Who's un-believably shallow and says rather a lot most of the time!'

Amy faltered, a little self-consciously. 'I – er – I'll tell Edmund that you're here...'

'Is this a weed, Amy?' called Vicky from

across the vegetable path where they were working, some days later. 'Shall I pull it up?'

'Yes – but remember to pull gently and try to get the root up.'

Amy sat back on her heels, pushing back her sun-bonnet from her damp forehead as Edmund sauntered into the garden grinning from ear to ear.

'How did you get on at Whiteladies?' she asked.

'Gilbert asked me lots of questions about the books he's lent me and we discussed all sorts of things. He really listened to what I had to say, as if my opinions were important,' replied Edmund, adding exuberantly, 'He said the paper I'd written on Virgil was already of a high standard and if I go on working hard I'll have an excellent chance of gaining the scholarship!'

'Well done!' Amy got to her feet and hugged him. 'That's wonderful!'

'He's lent me another batch of books and set me more exercises. I said we'd have our next meeting here. That was all right, wasn't it? Only I felt a bit awkward being up at Whiteladies,' he owned.

Amy bent to cut some beans for dinner. 'Yes, of course you must bring Mr Gilbert here for your discussions. You can take him into the sitting-room. You won't be disturbed there.'

'I met Gilbert's father,' went on Edmund. 'He was very polite, but I felt he thought Gilbert should be doing something more worthwhile with his time!'

'From what I've heard,' remarked Amy drily, 'Alfred Paslew regards anything not connected to making money as a waste of time.'

'I suppose so, but he didn't seem like the tyrant that lots of people paint him.'

'You were a guest in his home, Edmund. I daresay other folk see Mr Paslew in a very different light.'

'Perhaps you're right.' He paused, savouring the moment. 'I've something else to tell you, Amy. After I'd seen Gilbert, I went into town and, well, just come inside and I'll show you.'

Amy and Vicky hurried indoors after him, and there in the centre of the table sat a small blue-glass brooch shaped like a star, a ragdoll, and a little pile of coins.

'This is for you.' He gave Vicky the doll and she at once raced out into the garden with it. 'The brooch is yours, Amy. It reminded me of the Dog Star tale that you tell Vicky when Pa's away. And the money's for you, too. For the family, you know.'

Amy swallowed hard, tears springing to her eyes as she touched the brooch with her fingertips. 'I don't understand...'

'Working on Collie Barraclough's farm now and then is all right but I've been on the look-out for a more regular job.' Edmund's smooth face was bright with excitement. 'Dan Ainsworth's taken me on to help in the stables at The Mermaid! This is my first week's wages – in advance, because Dan reckons he can trust me!'

'Edmund, you can't do this!' exclaimed Amy. 'I appreciate it, but I told you when you wanted to help at Barracloughs that it could only be temporary.'

'I know what you told me, Amy, but I don't agree!' he returned hotly. 'I've proven I can do a day's work, and now I want a proper job!'

'Cleaning out the stalls at The Mermaid Inn?'

'What's wrong with that? Pa would say it's honest work!'

'Yes, I know he would. And it is,' she said, managing to keep her voice even, despite her growing anger. 'It isn't the job, Edmund, it's you! I don't want you working for pennies when you should be studying for your future!'

'What about what *I* want?' he demanded. 'I told Aunt Anne about it on my way from town and she thought it an admirable idea! She said I'll make far better progress studying on my own, away from school, now that Gilbert's helping and lending me the best books. Aunt Anne is even drawing up a timetable for me to follow. Everything will work out, you'll see!'

'No, Edmund. I understand you're disappointed, but it's for the best.'

'Best for whom?' he retorted stubbornly. 'If I want to get a job, I will!'

'Why can't you see how foolish it is to jeopardise your scholarship for a job in the stables? I won't allow you to do it!'

'You can't stop me!'

Snatching up his books and writing tablet, Edmund stormed from the cottage. Amy made to follow him into the garden, then stopped in her tracks. Perhaps it would be wiser to give him a little time alone? He was sure to see the sense of her decision when he calmed down.

With a sigh, she picked up the pretty little brooch. Resting it upon her palm, the clear blue glass caught the sunlight so it sparkled and glinted like a real star. Dear Edmund!

How like him to be so unselfish but it really wouldn't do.

Ruefully, she gathered up the scattered coins from the table and with a glance towards the garden where Edmund was sitting studying and Vicky playing with her new doll, Amy slipped away from the cottage.

She found Dan Ainsworth in the stables, repairing a bridle. It was quiet in there, and smelled of linseed, beeswax, and sweet summer hay. He glanced up in surprise when she walked in.

'Edmund's wages,' she said softly, setting down the coins upon the workbench. 'I'm sorry there's some missing. I'll make up the difference next week when I'm paid at Whiteladies.'

He raised his eyes to search Amy's solemn face. 'What's all this about?'

'I wish you hadn't offered him that job!' she burst out in dismay. 'I daresay you meant well–'

'I'm obliged for that small consideration!' he cut in sarcastically.

'Please don't be difficult, Dan! I've just had a row with Edmund, and all this unpleasantness could have been avoided if only you'd asked me first!'

His stony gaze held hers. 'Why would I do that?'

'Because you know I don't want him working!' she exclaimed impatiently. 'It's out of the question. He needs to concentrate upon preparing for his scholarship examination.'

'You need to get your facts straight, Amy. I didn't offer Edmund the job – although I would've, if I'd thought about it. He saw it chalked up on the board and of the lads who came in and asked, Edmund was the best.'

'He just saw the chance to earn some money; he doesn't realise his whole future is at stake!' she retorted angrily. 'For goodness' sake, he's just a boy.'

'You don't give Edmund the credit he's due,' returned Dan coldly. 'He's young, but there're lads his age and younger at the clay pits. Besides, Edmund's more of a man in his ways and his thoughts than plenty who are much older. Your brother Rory being a prime example.'

'Can't you understand–'

'It's you that doesn't understand! You don't want Edmund to get a job, so you knock him down and come running to me behind his back to return his wages! You're wrong, Amy! If you'd set out to humiliate the lad and rob him of his pride and self-respect, then you couldn't have done it any better!'

Amy stared into his accusing eyes, her anger and frustration draining from her. The stables were very quiet, yet the snuffle and whicker of horses, the rustling of dry hay and the soft whirr of swallows' wings as they flew amongst the beams in the loft were loud to Amy's ears.

'I hadn't... I didn't think about how it must seem from his point of view,' she mumbled unhappily, lowering her eyes. 'I wouldn't hurt Edmund for all the world–'

'I know that, and so does he,' interrupted Dan softly, going to her as she stood forlornly in a shaft of sunshine that filtered through the dusty glass panes. 'You try too hard, lass. Always thinking about what's best for others. Happen it's time you started thinking about yourself,' he murmured, gently drawing her close and lowering his lips towards her.

Hours later, after Amy's apologies were made to Edmund, and all was well again between her and her younger brother who was to work at The Mermaid with her blessing, she was alone at Clockmaker's Cottage polishing Ma's piano. While she worked, her thoughts were full of the remembrance of Dan's warm lips upon her own.

Gladys Braithwaite came downstairs after discussing the day's menus with Mrs Paslew, and bustled into the kitchen.

'Huh, seems they want a fancy dinner for tomorrow night – special guests!' she huffed. 'A bit more notice wouldn't have come amiss! Amy – make yourself presentable! The missus is wanting to see you in the drawing-room.'

'Why?' Amy spun around from the sink. 'Is something wrong?'

'How should I know? I'm not a mind-reader, am I?' The cook double-tied an apron about her ample middle. 'Look sharp, girl!'

Mrs Paslew was seated at the writing desk beside the drawing-room window.

'Amy! Come in.' She looked up from the letter in her hands. 'My daughters are going into Liverpool on Thursday in order to shop and to visit their dressmaker. They'll be putting up overnight and returning on the midday coach, next day. I'd like you to accompany them.'

Amy's thoughts were racing. Liverpool!

She'd never been away from Monks Quay before! And would Aunt Anne be able to stay at Clockmaker's Cottage while she was gone...?

'Thank you, ma'am.'

'I want you to do some shopping for me while you're there. I've made out a list. Most of the establishments are in Bold Street, so you shouldn't have any difficulty in finding them. I had intended to make the trip myself; however we have guests coming to stay and I'm needed here. There's something else, too.' Mrs Paslew smiled, and it seemed to Amy her whole face lit up with happiness. 'Our eldest daughter and her husband have written to tell us that we are to be grandparents for the first time! The baby won't arrive for some months, but I want you to make a complete set of everything that an infant requires, and you must embroider it all as beautifully as you did Clemmie's runner!'

'Yes, ma'am ... but,' began Amy, chewing her lips, 'I knew Miss Clemmie, ma'am! At least, I knew she was fond of the walled garden and I put that on her runner, but–'

'Of course! Gwendoline left Whiteladies long before you started working here. Now, what can I tell you about her tastes?' mused

Mrs Paslew with a thoughtful frown. 'Well, she loves children and music and, as a girl, adored drawing wild flowers. Indeed, that's how she met her husband – Simon is a botanist. Gwendoline is a keen gardener, too; it was she who planted and tended the herb garden – she never allowed Dobson or the garden boys anywhere near it while she was living here! I'm afraid I can't think of anything else, Amy.'

'I'm sure that'll be enough, ma'am.' In her mind's eye, Amy was already seeing how pretty a delicate pattern of herbs and wild flowers might look upon a baby's shawl and nightgowns, and suchlike.

'Splendid! You must make a list of the materials you'll need and purchase everything while you're in Liverpool. I shall have a word with Mrs Braithwaite, too. Although you'll continue to help her, you'll need plenty of time away from the kitchen to devote to your needlework. You may go now.' Eleanor Paslew picked up her letter once more. 'We'll have another talk before you leave for Liverpool.'

Impatient to share her news with Dan, Amy flew down the lane and flung herself into his arms the instant she spotted him coming towards the schoolhouse to meet her.

'Dan – I'm to go to Liverpool with the Paslew sisters! We're to stay at a hotel and I'm to go shopping in Bold Street! But, best of all, Mrs Paslew has asked me to embroider a layette for her first grandchild! I'm doing a pattern of wild flowers and herbs–' Becoming aware of the rigid set of his jaw, her words trailed off and she stepped back from him. 'Whatever is it, Dan? I was delighted to be asked to do it.'

'Aye, I can see that plain as day,' he answered grimly. 'It's bad enough you spending every hour God sends skivvying for the Paslews, without them piling on extra work and sending you away from your home to run errands for them!'

'I enjoy sewing and it'll be lovely making the baby things,' she replied, slipping her arm through his as they walked, with Vicky hopscotching ahead of them. 'I'm glad Mrs Paslew and Miss Clemmie think I'm a good needlewoman. It's nice having my work appreciated.'

'From where I stand, they're just taking advantage.'

'Don't be churlish! I thought you'd be pleased for me!'

'I'll not be pleased until the day you leave

Whiteladies Grange for good. I can't stomach the notion of you waiting on the Paslews hand and foot.'

'Well, I'm thrilled about all this! Mrs Paslew said I'm to spend less time in the kitchen to make more time for sewing – and I'd far rather sew than scour pots and pans for Gladys Braithwaite! And I'm looking forward to going to Liverpool. Aunt Anne will keep an eye on things at Clockmaker's Cottage, and I have to set off really early on Thursday morning because the coach comes–'

'I do know when the Liverpool coach comes through.' He sighed heavily. 'Liverpool's a long way off and you've not the slightest notion what you might be letting yourself in for.'

'I'm accompanying Miss Sophie and Miss Clemmie and doing some errands for Mrs Paslew,' she explained patiently. 'I'm also to buy whatever I need for the layette, from Mosleys' in Bold Street – that's the haberdashery where Mr Gilbert bought my silver scissors. Although Aunt Anne's never been to Liverpool, she's heard of Mosleys' and says it's the finest haberdashery in the whole of Lancashire.' She reached up to brush his rough cheek with a kiss. 'Why can't you be happy for me?'

'I can't be happy you're going away, Amy, even for just a day. I don't want you gallivanting with the likes of them. I want you here – with me!'

'Dan!'

Their tender kiss was interrupted by Vicky's shouting for them to hurry and catch up, because she couldn't clamber over the stile by herself.

'What's *he* been doing at Clockmaker's?' exclaimed Dan, spotting Gilbert Paslew cantering towards the bridle path that ran through Friars Wood.

'Who? Oh, Mr Gilbert? He'll have been helping Edmund with his studies. Aunt Anne says he's a first-rate scholar,' replied Amy matter-of-factly, bundling Vicky over the high, jagged stones of the sea-facing stile. 'Will you stay for supper tonight? I've made plum cobbler for afters.'

'Can't refuse that, can I?' He grinned, adding seriously, 'I wish you wouldn't go to Liverpool, Amy. It's a place like you can never even imagine until you actually see it. When I was about Edmund's age, I went a couple of times with Collie Barraclough's hay-cart – it's a huge, filthy, dark place! There's smoke and dirt and noise and people

– people crammed together on the streets so close you could scarce put a pin between then!' He shook his head in disgust. 'And the air's so foul, you're loath to breathe it!'

'That's not how Pa speaks of the town, and he often sails into there with the Jenet Rae,' remarked Amy. 'Aren't there fine buildings and grand shops and hotels and magnificent ships that sail around the whole world?'

'Aye, there's that and more. The town's got brass, no doubt about it,' he admitted. 'But next to the big houses and fancy carriages and concert halls, there's folk in rags and beggars on every corner. You must be on your guard every minute. The streets are teeming with vagabonds and cut-throats who prey on strangers.' Dan touched a hand to her cheek, meeting her gaze with trouble eyes. 'I mean it, Amy. You take care – great care. Liverpool's a dangerous place for a young lass alone.'

A Proposal

Upon her arrival in Liverpool, Amy found Dan's vivid description of the thriving port coming to life all around her.

Accustomed to Monks Quay, where open sea, meadow and woodland stretched as far as the eye could see and, even in the town, most faces were familiar, here Amy's senses were assaulted.

She felt swallowed up by walls and crowds that pressed in all about her.

Soot-blackened buildings towered high above the carriage as it crawled to the hotel along a maze of dark, cobbled streets crammed with vehicles of every kind, and seething with jostling, hurrying people – people of colours and costumes she'd never seen before, speaking in tongues and dialects foreign and rapid to her ears. Everywhere was noise, bustle and thick, choking chimney smoke!

At Clemmie's behest, Amy accompanied the sisters to the milliner but declined the opportunity to go with them to their dressmaker. Mindful of the list of errands she needed to complete for Mrs Paslew, she was anxious to be off and started.

She'd thought it gallant when Gilbert Paslew offered to escort her on her errands, but she was aware he was in Liverpool to conduct business for his father and besides, she was keen to prove herself capable of finding her own way and managing without help. She was also hoping to slip away down to the river and see all the magnificent ocean-going brigs and schooners and clippers and barques Pa had told her about!

How surprised and pleased he'd be when he brought the Jenet Rae home and Amy told him she'd been on a trip of her own!

As soon as Mrs Paslew's errands were done – the fabrics, silks, buttons and ribbons for the layette chosen and purchased, and arrangements made for the parcels and boxes to be promptly delivered to the hotel – Amy sought directions to the docks.

Acutely aware of Dan's warnings, and of the crush of people and traffic surging along the streets, she walked briskly through the town and soon glimpsed topsails in the near distance. Turning a sharp corner, the dull swell of murky waves lay before her and Amy gasped to see the scores of vessels – three, four, five abreast – at anchor, and the swarms of men, women, children, pack-horses, carts and barrows, milling like colonies of busy insects all along the waterfront.

She stood, drinking in every sight and sound so she might tell Edmund and Vicky, Aunt Anne and Pa, every last detail.

And she was taking a final look at it all when she suddenly saw Rory walking straight past her, not more than a few yards away. For a split-second, she just stared. He was already being absorbed by the crowd...

'Rory!' she called after him, but he did not turn around and she had to break into a run, grabbing at his arm when at last he was within her reach. 'Rory!'

'How did you find me?' He glared sharply at her, his shrewd eyes sliding beyond his sister to scan the mass of faces moving around them. 'Who's with you?'

'Nobody! Rory, you disappeared without a word. Are you all right? What are you doing here?'

'Working.' He spat out the words. 'What does it look like I'm doing?'

'Are you working for Theodore Buxton?' she asked quietly, noting his appearance for the first time. Although not as smartly dressed as Fanny had described, Rory was cleanly shaven, well-clad and had a certain air of authority in his bearing. 'Is that why you were in York recently? To see Theodore?'

'I don't know you, and you don't know me. Get it? Now, go on your way.' He started away from her without another glance. 'And do yourself a favour, Amy – don't look back!'

Despite the warmth of the day, a chill of foreboding shuddered the length of Amy's spine. Unsure of what to do next, she followed him at a distance, watching him shouldering his way through the crowds.

Presently he veered towards a massive, red-bricked, barn-like, sea-facing building six storeys high with row upon row of small windows along the uppermost floors. Here he paused, spoke briefly to an older man dressed in working clothes who was loading a wagon with kegs, then vanished within the dark confines of the cavernous building.

Amy slowly retraced her steps. What on earth was Rory doing in Liverpool? It was a long way from Monks Quay. And from York! If he and Theodore were still in league – and somehow, Amy was certain Rory was still working for Fanny's husband – what was it that they did? And how was Rory connected to that vast building on the waterfront?

An old seaman with only one leg was selling

newspapers outside a chandlery. He probably knew everyone and everything that passed him by. Amy stopped, politely enquiring about the building Rory had entered.

'Customs warehouse, miss.' The sailor tapped snuff on to the back of his hand and inhaled. 'Full to the rafters with ships' cargo. Can't come out till the duty gets paid on it, see?'

Amy didn't, but she would ask Dan about it later.

'What sorts of goods are kept in there?'

'Want to know a lot, don't you?' He squinted up at her suspiciously. 'Fancy stuff, that's what. Brandy, rum, tea, spices and all such else – now do you want to buy a paper or not?'

Clutching a newspaper, and suddenly aware of the lateness of the afternoon, Amy sped from the river, up through the town to the hotel. She'd been far longer than she'd intended and worried lest the Paslew sisters had returned and were angrily waiting for her to attend them.

She need not have been concerned, for when she hurried, flushed and breathless, into the hotel lobby, Gilbert Paslew rose from one of the sofas and immediately set her mind at ease.

'No sign of my sisters yet!' He smiled, offering Amy his arm. 'Looks as though we'll have to go to tea without them!'

'I can't do that!' she cried without thinking, catching her breath and straightening her bonnet. 'I'll have to see to them when they get back and–'

'It would be an act of compassion, Miss MacFarlane,' he went on, firmly propelling her towards the brass and mahogany revolving doors. 'After a day spent negotiating contracts with various unscrupulous individuals, I'm sorely in need of civilised companionship, together with a pot of fine tea and a substantial plate of madeleines. Rather than here at the hotel, I recommend we take refreshment at a very pleasant teashop not far from the library. Then perhaps a stroll through the gardens? There's often a band playing there. You do like music, don't you?' And he swept her out into the late afternoon sunshine.

'Mr Gilbert!' Amy began, aware of his hand resting lightly upon her arm to keep her at his side. 'I can't just... What about Miss Clemmie and Miss Sophie?'

He shrugged. 'Let them get their own tea and madeleines!'

It was a lovely afternoon. Tea. The band

playing. Walking with Gilbert through the gardens. Amy hadn't given another thought to her encounter with Rory, nor even to what repercussions there might be with the Misses Paslew, until they were entering the hotel once more.

Then the carefree happiness of the afternoon seemed to melt away into the dusk, and – suddenly feeling very much the servant again – she was anxious to return to where she belonged and moved from his side, lowering her eyes.

'Thank you for tea,' she murmured awkwardly.

'The thanks are all mine, Miss Mac-Farlane. I can't recall when I've enjoyed an afternoon more.' Touching a hand to her elbow, he accompanied her to the sweeping staircase. 'I suppose I'd better look in on my sisters – by the way, you will join us for dinner this evening, won't you?'

'No!' she exclaimed in horror, adding quietly, 'It wouldn't be appropriate.'

'We aren't in the autocratic realm of Whiteladies Grange now!' he declared dismissively. 'And you'll have to eat, anyway, won't you? I'll call for you at eight and we'll all go down together.'

The prospect of dining with the Paslews in

a grand hotel was not one Amy looked forward to. Even wearing her best dress, she felt homely and horribly out of place until Clemmie slipped her arm through hers and the two girls descended the staircase together.

It was a fine meal with much lively conversation and laughter. After relating a humorous incident that had occurred at the glover's, the irrepressible Sophie launched into a description of her plans for captivating Laurence Deane when he and Amelia came to stay at Whiteladies Grange later that month.

'...and Gilbert, I shall be relying upon you to entertain Amelia.'

'I can't. I'll be bookkeeping for Father's brick kilns on that day.'

'Which day?' challenged Sophie.

'Whichever day you want me to entertain Amelia Deane!'

'Gilbert, if you don't help me woo Laurence, then I'll become an old maid, and because brothers are duty-bound to provide for their spinster sisters, you'll have me living with you for the rest of your life!'

'Good Lord! Anything but that!' Gilbert grimaced, catching Amy's eye.

'That's settled then.' Lowering her voice, Sophie looked around the table conspiratorially. 'I have a wooing plan, and it's absolutely foolproof...'

It was very late when Amy climbed into bed in the bare little room that had been set aside at the end of the corridor for hotel guests' maids, boot boys and valets. It had been quite a day and she slept almost at once, her last waking thought being of seeing Dan again tomorrow.

'Well done, everyone! That was a fine effort – especially from the trebles!'

All Hallows' weekly choir practice was drawing to a close and the Reverend William Linley leaned heavily on his cane, glancing benignly towards the fidgeting little boys in the front row who were longingly eyeing the sunshine beyond the open west door.

'I just have a short announcement to make. You'll be relieved to know that instead of having to put up with me muddling my way through the sheet music, you're to once more have a proper choirmaster! I've twisted my nephew's arm and he's agreed to step into the breach. Gilbert?'

Along with the rest of the choir, Amy watched Gilbert Paslew make his way from the rear of the stalls down to Reverend Linley's side.

'I'm proud to have been asked to become choirmaster, and I'll do my very best to be a good one.' Gilbert smiled across at the singers, his quiet voice resonating a round the centuries-old church. 'Of course, I'll still be singing with you and playing the organ whenever it's my turn to do so.

'Now, although harvest festival is still a while off, I'm already planning the music for our service of thanksgiving and, as harvest approaches, please remember to give as much as you're able for those less fortunate than ourselves. Whether it be food, fuel, warm clothing or other comforts. And, as usual, we'll require help to deliver baskets to the needy after the harvest festival is over. We'll begin rehearsals for the service next week,' concluded Gilbert, his face breaking into a warm smile. 'Meanwhile, I'll see you all bright and early on Sunday morning!'

The choir dispersed and everyone began to leave the church.

Gilbert and Reverend Linley were talking quietly beside the pulpit and as Amy went by, the vicar called out to her.

'Amy! Can you spare a few minutes?' he asked hopefully. 'Will you come with me to the rectory? Mrs Linley – well, both of us, really – would like to ask you something.'

The vicar started towards the vestry, his steps slow and awkward, and Amy followed.

'Sounds important.' Gilbert smiled as she passed him. 'Good luck!'

'The vicar and Mrs Linley have asked me to start a Sunday school,' Amy told Dan. They were apple-picking in the little mixed orchard beyond Clockmaker's Cottage. 'When we were young, Mrs Linley took Sunday school. After she became poorly, it stopped.'

'I wouldn't know,' he commented from the top of the ladder. 'I never went.'

'Fancy them asking me to run it!'

'And you said you would?'

'Of course I did! Sunday school is very important! It's a lovely way for the little ones to learn. I'm making a start next week.'

'It's nice you were asked,' he conceded. 'But Sunday is the only time you get a few hours away from Whiteladies Grange. Now you won't even have that time to yourself because you'll be at the church all day long.'

'I want to take the classes, Dan!' she cried in surprise, craning her neck to look up at him. 'It's not a chore!'

'And what about you and me, Amy?' he responded, unhooking the apple-bag from across his chest. 'When is there going to be

140

time for us to be together?'

'We see each other lots!' Taking the weight of the bag, she laid it on to the grass and knelt to begin sorting the fruit. 'And we spend nice days like this together.'

'We see each other, aye, but...' Dan's gaze drifted the length of the orchard with its mature trees that bore plums, damsons and pears as well as apples, where Amy's brother and sister and Nicholas Buxton were also picking fruit, and decided to change the subject altogether.

'You told Edmund about meeting Rory in Liverpool, then? He mentioned it last night at The Mermaid.'

Amy nodded, arranging the apples carefully in the trug so they wouldn't bruise. 'I thought long and hard about it. In the end, I just said I'd seen Rory and spoken to him. Nothing more. I don't want Edmund to know anything about his brother's wrongdoing, but it's dreadful keeping things from him.'

'Maybe so,' he replied, climbing up into the boughs. 'But it'd do Edmund no good to know what we know, so why give him the burden of it?'

She straightened up, arching her aching back. 'That's true. I'm guilty and ashamed because I know it was Rory who attacked Sydney Wallace and yet I did nothing to bring about justice. I don't ever want Edmund to feel this way.'

'You're not to blame, Amy. There's only one who is, and he won't be losing any sleep over it!'

'What do you suppose Rory and Theodore are up to in Liverpool? Have you heard anything? News coming in with the coach, I mean?'

'Nowt in particular,' he answered. 'A man like Buxton has all the right connections. It'd be my guess he does the organising from a gentlemanly distance, while Rory's down in the thick of it. He's a hard man, your brother. There's not many who'd be willing to cross him.'

'Especially when he's carrying a pistol,' she murmured grimly. 'And Rory told me he was working!'

'Thieving, more like!' Dan returned scornfully. 'The old sailor said it was a customs' warehouse didn't he? All sorts of valuable cargo gets stored in those places. Just there for the taking! Rory and Buxton are likely getting rich selling stolen goods to wealthy folk who'll happily turn a blind eye to avoid paying the government its duty!'

'Rory will go to gaol if he's caught, won't he?' she said bleakly. 'Or face transportation.'

'They're playing a dangerous game, Amy. Gambling on being too clever to get caught,' replied Dan. 'But who knows? Maybe Rory and Buxton are slippery enough to get away with it.'

He looked across the orchard to where Nicholas Buxton was picking damsons.

'Do you reckon he knows anything about all this?'

'I doubt it very much. Nick's a decent sort,' she responded, following his gaze. 'He's a kind man and he thinks about other people, which is more than can be said for his older brother – or mine!'

Vicky ran over, the damson basket clutched in both arms and her bonnet askew. 'I've picked lots, Amy! Can we bake a pie, now? Can we? And have it for tea?'

'Apple and damson pie would go down well, Amy!' chipped in Edmund from the heights of his pear tree.

'Just the job after spending a whole day picking the dratted things,' agreed Dan. 'What do you say, Amy?'

'On one condition.' She was looking towards Nicholas. 'Vicky and I will make a pie if Nick promises to stay and share it!'

'Rather!' he exclaimed, pleased. 'You're the best cook in the whole world, Amy – heaps better than Mrs Braithwaite at White-ladies!'

'That's settled, then.' Straightening Vicky's bonnet, she picked up her trug of apples. 'Come on, Vicky – we've a pie to bake!'

Hand in hand, the sisters walked through the orchard towards Clockmaker's Cottage, leaving the men to their labours.

It was a warm afternoon, and Amy had conducted her first Sunday school class beneath the shady trees that grew beside the north transept. She was clearing up when Gilbert Paslew came across from the rectory.

'May I help?' He stopped and started to gather up slates and books without waiting for an answer. 'How did it go?'

'It went well, I think!' She laughed, crossing her fingers.

'From what I saw, it was a great success!' he responded, following her into the church. 'The children were utterly absorbed when you were reading to them.'

'The Parable Of The Good Shepherd.' She smiled, stacking the books into the cupboard. 'Aren't you very early for evensong?'

'I'm thinking of introducing a little of Mozart's sacred music into the service. However, since I haven't played any for a while, I decided a practice would be a sensible idea!' He leafed through the sheet music he'd brought with him. 'Will you tell me what you think? About my playing, and whether you think this piece suitable for evensong?'

'Gladly. And if it's anything like the music you were playing when Reverend and Mrs Linley were at Whiteladies the other evening, I'm sure it will suit perfectly well.' She glanced up at him, her warm brown eyes dancing. 'Although you do realise some of the congregation will be up in arms because it's different?'

'Ah!' He nodded gravely. 'Well, the worst that can happen is my being struck off the organ-playing rota and banished from Monks Quay,' he replied, adding, 'which reminds me; Nicholas asked me to tell you he'll call at Clockmaker's Cottage after supper tonight to say his goodbyes.'

Amy nodded. 'His coach leaves at first light tomorrow. Nick's really become part of the family; we're all going to miss him – especially Vicky. She loves having another big brother to play games with!'

'Nicholas mentioned something about collecting a box, too. He said you'd understand?'

'I do. Nick's taking letters from us all, and a box of jams and bottled fruit, back to York with him for Fanny. I don't suppose she does her own baking any more, so I'm sending her a plum cake and an apple pie as well.'

'You miss your sister a great deal, don't you?'

'Mmm. We write regularly, but it isn't the same as talking to her.'

'Why don't you go with Nicholas to York tomorrow?' Gilbert exclaimed impulsively. 'You could visit your sister for a while!'

'Go to York?' she echoed, astonished. 'How could I do that?'

'I'm sure your aunt would look after Vicky,' he went on enthusiastically. 'And a leave of absence from Whiteladies Grange can easily be arranged.'

'No!' she cried, shaking her head. 'No, Gilbert. I couldn't!'

'All you need do is pack and board the coach,' he persisted amiably. 'I'll arrange it all and pay your fare.'

'You don't see...' She frowned, unable to explain. 'It wouldn't – it wouldn't be right!'

'Amy – I'm sorry!' He spoke earnestly, reaching out and catching her fingers, holding her still when she would have moved away from him. 'I didn't mean to offend you!'

Involuntarily, Amy gasped. Her eyes were drawn to their joined hands.

Following her gaze, Gilbert gently released her.

'I believed we had become friends, Amy.' His grey eyes were solemn. 'I would very much have liked to give this small happiness to you.'

The next morning, Amy decided to leave Clockmaker's Cottage earlier than usual so that she could see Nick off before going on to Whiteladies Grange. Gilbert Paslew had ridden into town with him, and the two men were already at The Mermaid when she arrived. It was chilly, and they ushered her inside to the warmth of the inn's blazing fire.

'I can't tell you what it's meant to me to feel part of a real family these past months!' said Nicholas. 'I understand how you feel about Monks Quay – if it were my home, I'd never want to leave, either!'

Amy swallowed hard. 'Come back soon!'

she told him.

The horn blew, and they went out into the damp, misty morning and saw the coach making ready to leave. Dan had harnessed fresh horses and was helping the driver load the last of the baggage.

Nicholas climbed aboard, settling into his seat.

'I'll be sure to give Fanny your box the moment I get to Carteret Square!'

Amy returned his wave as the coach rattled away at a cracking pace.

'You don't have to be up at Whiteladies for a while yet,' Dan said, striding across the cobbles to her. 'Come in for some chocolate. There's a real nip in the air today!'

'Autumn's not far off,' she replied, glancing back to Gilbert. 'Are you coming in?'

'I don't think so.'

'I'm glad you weren't pilloried for the Mozart.'

'It's early days yet!' He grinned, mounting his bay horse. 'I'll see you at choir practice – all being well!'

The inn was unusually peaceful and quiet. It was still too early for any guests to be up and about, and the next coach wasn't due for another couple of hours. Dan and Amy sat together companionably at the fireside; warmth and silence enveloping them as they sipped the steaming cups of strong chocolate.

'It could always be like this for us, if we were wed,' he murmured.

'Dan?' She twisted around on the settle to face him.

'I mean it. Let's get married.'

'Married... I've never even thought... Well, not really,' she got out at length. 'Anyway, I can't get married. Not yet.'

'Because of the family? I know you've them to think about but that's no reason not to get married,' he went on practically. 'You can be my wife and still look after them! Your da's at sea most of the time and Edmund'll be going away once he gets his scholarship. That just leaves Vicky, and she's a grand little lass.'

'I can't marry you, Dan. It isn't the family – it's me,' she whispered, unable to meet his yes. 'I care for you very much. You're my best friend in all the world ... but ... I'm so sorry,' she faltered miserably, finally raising her gaze to his. 'I'm just not sure enough of my feelings.'

'That's all right, lass. I'm sure of mine for you.' He drew her closer into his arms. 'And I shall go on asking you until you say yes!'

A few days later, Amy sat down to write to Fanny. Clockmaker's Cottage was uncomfortably hot, and she'd left Edmund studying with Gilbert Paslew in the sitting-room, and had taken her writing tablet into the garden. It was no cooler out there. Not a breath of breeze was coming in from the sea. The sky was low and white and the air sultry.

'*Dan has asked me to marry him,*' she wrote. '*You've often teased me about Dan, and how I should snap him up the first chance I get, but I couldn't accept his proposal. I think I must love him a little, because I'm happy whenever we're together and I don't know what I'd do without him. But is that true love, Fanny?*

You were so sure about Theodore! But I don't know if marrying Dan would be the right thing to do. If only I could see you and talk to you about all this! Oh! You'll never guess what happened the day before Nick left for York! Out of the blue, Gilbert Paslew said he'd get me a seat on the coach so I could go with Nick and visit you!

I was quite shocked at first, then I was very tempted! Obviously, it was out of the question. I realise Gilbert meant it kindly and honourably, but it would've been improper for me to accept a favour of that sort, don't you think? And can you imagine what Pa would say when he came ashore and found out? He'd be furious! Pa'd think it the most awful insult to me, and to the family.

You know how bitter he feels towards the Paslews. He even disapproves of Gilbert helping Edmund with his scholarship work, although it isn't fair for him to have a grudge against Gilbert simply because he's Albert Paslew's son.

Amy sat on the parched grass beneath the apple tree, her head bowed over the writing tablet that rested upon her lap. The afternoon was growing hotter and ever more oppressive. By and by, perspiration trickled down her forehead and neck, and just as Edmund and Gilbert emerged from Clockmaker's Cottage, there came the distant grumbling of thunder, far out to sea.

Edmund had been rather low in spirits of late, and Amy had wondered if his studies and the stable-work at The Mermaid were becoming too much for him. However, he looked much brighter today.

Setting aside her letter to finish later, Amy smiled up at him as he and Gilbert approached. 'How are you getting on?'

'Better! And not before time!' He grinned at her. 'I've been struggling with Latin for weeks and weeks, but at long last it is starting to make sense.'

'Well done! All your efforts are bringing good results.'

'Anne was absolutely right about your brother,' put in Gilbert, offering his hand to help her rise from the grass. 'He does have outstanding ability. However, that alone counts for little without the will to work hard and persevere even when the task seems impossible. The scholarship examination won't have a worthier candidate, nor one more deserving of the award.'

'I've still a long way to go before the examination,' commented Edmund sensibly, trying not to look too pleased. 'Are you both off to choir practice now?'

Amy and Gilbert set off across the meadows.

'Now that we've had a few rehearsals,' Amy said as they strolled through the tinder-dry, knee-high grasses. 'The choir is starting to get a feel for the music. And it's a nice change to have the youngest children singing a few hymns on their own.'

'Yes, they do seem to like doing that, don't they?' he commented. 'It was hearing the little ones singing at your Sunday school that gave me the idea–'

A shuddering growl of thunder, followed by a sky-splitting crack of lightning, drowned his words.

Then the heavens opened and the storm broke.

Dragging off his coat, Gilbert wrapped it tightly about Amy's shoulders.

Rain was coursing down his face and she knew he was shouting but she couldn't hear a word, so loud was the sound of the rain.

With an arm securely about her waist, he pointed across the meadow and, with heads bowed into the driving rain, they ran for Pargetter's barn.

Soaked to the skin and breathless, they burst through the broken timber doors. Apart from a few bales of old, sorry-looking hay, a rusting plough and various other forgotten tools, the barn was empty and hadn't seen use or repair since old Miss Pargetter's brother passed away.

The broken roof leaked like a sieve, and they weren't much drier inside.

'But I suppose it's better than standing under a tree!' commented Gilbert, watching a brilliant fork of lightning snaking across the leaden sky. 'If the whole place doesn't collapse around us, we should be fine.'

Amy laughed, but couldn't stop shaking.

The temperature was plummeting and she was wet through, her sodden clothing clinging to her cold skin.

'You're shivering–' Gilbert pulled the coat tighter about her, taking her white hands into his own and rubbing them vigorously. 'Any better?'

'Much, thank you.'

He didn't release her. Murmuring her name, his grey eyes lingered upon her face and lips. 'Amy, I...'

Her heart was pounding so hard she couldn't breathe. She could only stand there, gazing up at him while the storm raged all around. Then a rapid explosion of lightning illuminated the shadowy barn and jolted Amy back to her senses.

'I think the rain is stopping,' she said. 'We ought to go ... or we'll be late.'

The drenched meadow was sparkling in the watery sunlight when they emerged from the barn and continued onwards to All Hallows. With Gilbert's coat still around her, Amy was trembling, her legs weak at the knees. From time to time, she cast a glance towards the man walking at her side.

They hadn't spoken since leaving their shelter, but somehow it was perfectly companionable silence. When he held open the west door for her to enter the church, she looked up at him, their eyes meeting for the first time.

Suddenly, her pulse was racing and her senses flooded with new awareness. Dan had asked her to marry him. She couldn't imagine being without him and yet ... and yet, since those treacherous moments in Pargetter's barn, she'd been aching for Gilbert Paslew's kiss.

She had no notion of whether she sang the correct words during choir practice, or even if she sang in tune. Such was her distraction, she could only think of Gilbert – and the surge of emotion he'd stirred within her.

When she would usually have paused to speak with him after practice ended, this evening she was relieved to see another member of the choir engaging him with some question or other. Slipping away un-noticed, she wondered if he felt as she did and if her longings had been laid bare for him to see when they'd stood at the church door and he'd looked into her eyes.

The air had freshened somewhat since the storm and, stepping out into the cool twi-light, Amy scurried down the path from All Hallows. She was too absorbed in her thoughts to notice the figure waiting within the lychgate, and she started violently when Dan suddenly stepped out on to the path in front of her, his face angry and resentful.

'I saw you!' He caught her arm, hauling her into the confines of the ancient gateway. 'I saw you with him!'

Amy's heart was thumping in her chest. 'What – what do you mean?'

'You know full well!' he retorted, his eyes boring into her. 'I planned to meet you on your way to choir, but I was late. Then I spotted the pair of you running into Pargetter's barn – and saw him, with his hands on you! Deny it, Amy! Deny it if you can!'

'It wasn't like that!' she cried vehemently. 'The storm started suddenly and Gilbert lent me his coat and we sheltered in the barn – that's all!'

'Then marry me, Amy,' he mumbled thickly, pulling her hard against him. 'I'm done with waiting, lass – marry me now!'

A Hazardous Future

Amy was hurrying along Abbotsgate and had just passed The Mermaid Inn when Edmund sprinted out from the archway and ran after her.

'What are you doing in town?' he asked, catching her up.

'Collecting a book and some stationery that Miss Clemmie ordered from Jessups'. Are you finished for the day?'

'Almost–' he broke off as Dan crossed Abbotsgate from the other side and strode towards them, in the direction of the inn.

'Hello, Dan,' Amy said quietly as he drew level with them.

'Amy.' He nodded curtly, going past them into the inn yard.

Edmund looked from Dan's rigid back to his sister's dismayed face.

'Have you two fallen out? What's going on?'

'Nothing.'

'Something's happened. I have to work with him every day, and Dan's like a bear with a sore head,' persisted Edmund. 'He hasn't been to Clockmaker's for ages, and he barely spoke to you just now!'

Amy hesitated, her eyes as bleak as the dull sky. 'Dan asked me to marry him.'

'And you said no?' her brother exclaimed incredulously. 'But you and he – I thought you were bound to get married!'

'I'll see you at home tonight.'

'Wait–' Pulling a letter from his coat, Edmund offered it to her. 'From Fanny. It came on this morning's coach. That's why I called after you in the first place – and I think you made a mistake, refusing Dan!'

Amy shrugged, and went on her way. She'd always relished going into Jessups'. It was a cluttered little shop wedged between the apothecary and the dusty offices of Seward and Seward, where generations of Sewards had drawn up wills, deeds and contracts for the inhabitants of Monks Quay.

While Mr Jessup wrapped Clemmie Paslew's book and stationery, Amy browsed shelves filled with paint brushes, watercolours, charcoal sticks, pens, writing tablets, wafers, sealing wax and bottles of ink.

Outside once more, she wondered if there was time to take a cup of tea and read Fanny's letter before she made her way back to Whiteladies Grange. It was set to be another long day, for Miss Sophie's special guests had arrived earlier in the week. The entire household was on pins over this visit from Amelia and Laurence Deane, and Amy had already been scolded several times by Gladys Braithwaite for spending too much time sewing and not enough in the kitchen.

Now, with Fanny's long-awaited letter in her hand, she pushed open the curtained door of Betty Bower's tearoom. Going down the three uneven steps, she had just sat down at a corner table when the door bell jingled and she glanced up to see Gilbert Paslew raise his hat and come inside, bowing his head to avoid the low beams.

'May I join you? Oh, I beg your pardon—' He noticed the unopened letter in her hands. 'I'm disturbing you!'

'Not at all! I'll read it later – it's from Fanny.'

'That reminds me, I must write to Nicholas this week!' He sat down, ordering a pot of tea, oat cakes and white cheese. 'I'm hungry! I missed breakfast – well, actually, I escaped it! I really will be relieved when Amelia Deane and her brother go home!'

'Are they enjoying their visit?' asked Amy, pouring the tea.

'Absolutely! Laurence has had a serious talk with Father, so it appears Sophie's plan was indeed successful.' He smiled at her over the rim of his teacup. 'We had a very pleasant time in Liverpool, didn't we?'

'Oh, yes! For once, I'll have something interesting to tell Pa when he comes ashore!'

'When is he due home?'

'In another week or so. However, at this time of year, weather and tides can be very unpredictable,' explained Amy. 'If the Jenet Rae isn't able to make the crossing, she'll have to wait in Ireland until conditions improve enough to set sail.'

'I'm afraid I don't know much about the packet. But it must on occasion be very worrying for you. Your father has a dangerous occupation.'

'It can be. But Pa loves the sea. Without the sea and his boat, he'd be–' She broke off, blushing a little. 'Like a fish out of water! The sea is Pa's whole life. Always has been.'

'I envy – admire – somebody who has a real vocation,' reflected Gilbert seriously. 'My father certainly has – he thrives upon conducting business! I've spent the whole of today ensconced with young Mr Seward poring over all sorts of legal matters connected with Father's various business interests.' He offered Amy an oatcake. 'Small wonder I'm in need of sustenance! Another pot of tea?'

She shook her head. 'I really need to get on.'

'Me too.' He grimaced. 'I'm riding over to the brick kilns – Amy, have you been into the stationer's lately?'

'Just.'

'Did you read the notice about the play? Marlowe's Company of Players are coming to Monks Quay and putting on *She Stoops To Conquer*. Do you know it?'

'I haven't been to many plays. Is it good?'

'I think you'd enjoy it. It's a very witty play, but it says something serious at the same time. Would you like to go, Amy? Go with me, I mean?'

'Oh, yes!' she responded without thinking. 'Very much!'

'Splendid!' His grey eyes lit with pleasure. 'I'm sure we'll have a fine evening! I will be in touch once I've made all the arrangements.'

After Gilbert had taken his leave, Amy lingered a few minutes more in the tearoom and opened Fanny's letter.

After reading only a paragraph or two, she

gasped in delight.

'I'm not certain, Amy, so please do not breathe a word to a living soul; however, I really cannot imagine any other cause for my current symptoms other than that I am expecting a child. When Nicholas returned from Monks Quay, I was in floods of tears! Opening your box of treats left me quite undone! This isn't like me at all, Amy, and I'm feeling very impatient with myself!

However, I was immensely relieved to see Nicholas home again. I haven't been able to speak to Theo yet about my condition. He is away on business so frequently, and I miss him dreadfully. I now realise how hard it must've been for Ma, spending so much time parted from Pa while he was at sea. I confess to great loneliness in this fine big house, and wish with all my heart to be again part of the homely bustle of Clockmaker's Cottage. There! I never imagined I would ever say that!'

Amy's joy at the prospect of Fanny becoming a mother was tempered by concern for her sister's well-being. An impulsive notion of travelling to York, gradually strengthened with the passing days into firm resolve.

'I won't go until Pa comes ashore,' she told

Edmund. 'And I'll have to beg a leave of absence from Whiteladies, of course, but I don't think Mrs Paslew will refuse me.'

'Is Fanny ill?' Edmund's deepening voice registered alarm.

Amy hesitated. Although mindful of Fanny's request, she needed to reassure her young brother. 'Fanny might be expecting, and she isn't feeling very well. It's natural, and nothing to be concerned about, but I think she needs me. I'd really like to see her, too.'

'Can we afford it?'

'It'll mean emptying the caddy.'

'Is there enough in there?' Edmund glanced at Ma's old tea caddy, where the family saved whatever money they could spare. 'I bet the coach won't be cheap!'

'It isn't. I asked Mr Ainsworth.'

'Not Dan?' queried Edmund with a frown.

'Not Dan,' she replied flatly, meeting the reproof in Edmund's eyes. 'I now know for certain I could never marry him, but Dan still means so very much to me. I wish there wasn't this awful coldness between us. I'd thought – hoped – we could've…'

'Gone on as before?'

'Remained friends.'

'I see Dan every day, Amy. I see how angry

and hurt he is,' commented Edmund quietly. 'You really can't expect him to pretend he doesn't still love you when he plainly does.'

Poor weather delayed Ramsay MacFarlane by four days from bringing the Jenet Rae into Monks Quay, and Amy was greatly relieved when she heard that the packet had tied up and that Pa and his four crewmen were safely ashore. For no reason Amy could pin down, she'd felt a great uneasiness about this trip.

It had been Edmund who'd run from the inn to Whiteladies with the news that Pa was home.

'According to Ned Yarkin,' Edmund told Amy, 'Alfred Paslew and old Mr Seward were dining together at The Mermaid when word came that the Jenet Rae was coming in. Mr Paslew went down to the quayside to meet the packet and he and Pa came back up to The Mermaid together. They're still there now!'

'How odd!' considered Amy. It wasn't like Alfred Paslew to show any interest in the Jenet Rae at all, much less meet her at the quay!

'Something must be wrong. Did Mr Paslew seem annoyed?'

'No. Old Mr Seward was with them, too. They just looked like they were having an important conversation.'

'I don't know what to make of it,' Amy replied with a shake of her head. 'Thank you for coming to tell me that Pa's back. What with the bad weather and everything...'

'I know,' he said, adding hesitantly, 'It was Dan who suggested I come and give you the news. He still really cares about you, Amy.'

'And I for him, but not in the way he wishes me to. I expect I'll be late tonight. The Paslews are having another dinner party.'

It *was* late when Amy arrived home, and she was surprised to find Pa, Edmund and Aunt Anne too, all waiting up for her.

'I wanted to get the whole family to-gether,' began Ramsay, as soon as Amy was sitting down to her hotpot supper. 'I've something important to say... Alfred Paslew reckons he's neither the time nor the inclin-ation to keep the packet going. He wants shot of her.'

'What about you, Pa?' Amy was first to respond. 'And the crew?'

'Will the new owner keep you all on?' chipped in Edmund. 'Or will he bring in his own master and crew?'

'Steady now, we're getting ahead of ourselves here.' Ramsay raised a hand. 'There's no new owner. Not yet, at any rate.'

'Out with it, Ramsay,' said Anne a mite suspiciously. 'Tell us the worst!'

He drew in a measured breath before speaking. 'Paslew's offered me first refusal on the Jenet Rae – and I've said I'll think on it.'

'He's done what?' demanded Anne in disbelief. 'The gall of the man! You've been complaining for months that the boat is scarcely seaworthy, and now Alfred Paslew is generously letting you take her off his hands – providing you pay good money for the privilege! Small wonder he's the richest man in Monks Quay.'

She fixed her brother-in-law with a keen gaze.

'You're surely not seriously considering it, Ramsay? It's sheer foolishness!'

'Begging your pardon, Anne, but I disagree,' he replied quietly. 'The Jenet Rae isn't as shipshape as she might be, but she's a well-built vessel and stout at heart. There's nowt wrong with her that can't be put right.'

'At what cost?' challenged Anne. 'I notice Alfred Paslew hasn't spent a farthing more

166

than necessary on her!'

'That's true,' admitted Ramsay. 'Nor, in my opinion, did he ever have any proper interest in running the packet. Paslew has so many irons in the fire making huge profits for him, he's no time for the Jenet Rae. Happen she's more trouble than she's worth to him, but to me...'

'What, Pa?' prompted Amy gently, glimpsing the wistfulness in her father's expression. 'You want to buy her, don't you?'

'Aye, lass. Aye, I do,' he almost whispered, not meeting anyone's eyes. 'My whole life, I've doffed my cap and taken orders from whoever pays my wages – and been glad to do it. But I've looked at them that pays me as different and better, and I've envied them for it. For the first time, I've the opportunity to be my own boss and to make a secure future for my family.' Ramsay met Anne's gaze steadily. 'I don't want to let this chance pass me by, for at my time of life I'll surely never get another like it.'

'As owner, you would bear the entire responsibility for repairing, maintaining and sailing the vessel, as well as for paying the crew and supporting your own family!' returned Anne curtly. 'From what I hear, the packet is hardly a thriving concern with

Alfred Paslew behind it – why do you believe you can prosper where he does not?'

'Because I care about the Jenet Rae – and I need to make her prosper! What'll become of me when I'm too old to sail, if I don't have anything put by?' He went on earnestly, 'I've little enough learning, but I know the sea. I understand weather and tides and cargos in ways Paslew has no inkling of! Over the years, I've seen how the packet could be run better and told Paslew so, but he took no heed. I know I can make a go of it, Anne. All I'm asking is the chance to do it.'

They stared at one another across the table, the only sound the shifting of glowing coals in the kitchen hearth.

Amy glanced from her aunt's grimly set face to Pa's anxious one. She didn't understand why he was so desperately seeking Aunt Anne's approval.

'I'm sorry, Ramsay. The risks are too great,' said Anne at last. 'As you are aware, I intend leaving the few material goods in my possession to Amy. I cannot – will not – risk losing everything by supporting this whim of yours. For should this scheme fail, all would be lost!'

Anne Shawcross said goodnight and swept

from the cottage.

'That's that, then.' Ramsay expelled a slow breath, rubbing the palms of his callused hands over his face. 'In all fairness, I can't say I blame your aunt for deciding as she has. It must seem a crackpot scheme for the likes of me to run my own boat.'

'It doesn't!' exclaimed Amy, glancing quickly to Edmund, who nodded immediately. 'Edmund and I think you should buy the packet!'

'Thanks. Both of you. But I can't do it,' Ramsay said simply. 'I've no money. The only way would've been to put up the cottage.'

'Sell Clockmaker's?' cried Amy.

'Nay, it wouldn't be sold,' explained Ramsay. 'Old Mr Seward was there when I was talking to Paslew, and he said if I put up Clockmaker's Cottage as security, I could borrow enough money to buy the packet. It seemed a fair arrangement to me, and I told him so.' He glanced to his son and daughter. 'Thing is, Clockmaker's isn't mine to do what I like with.'

'Not yours? But–'

'It's straightforward enough, lass.' Ramsay sighed. 'I've hardly ever had a spare pound to my name, nor owned anything, either! Your ma and Aunt Anne inherited Clockmaker's Cottage from their parents who'd already passed away when I met and married your mother. Anne moved into the school-house so we could have the cottage to ourselves, but she still owns half of it.' He rose stiffly. 'I'm off to bed. Don't stay up too late, the pair of you.'

Brother and sister remained seated at the table.

'That explains a lot,' commented Edmund at length. 'I mean, we've never had much money, have we? Yet Clockmaker's is a very nice cottage. With the garden and orchard and things.'

'I just took our home for granted, I suppose,' Amy said. 'Poor Pa! What can we do?'

'You could try talking to Aunt Anne,' he suggested awkwardly. 'After all, she did say she was leaving everything to you. So if it's going to be yours one day anyway–'

'Edmund! Honestly!'

'I know. I'm sorry. I just couldn't think of anything else,' he admitted, shamefaced. 'Perhaps when Aunt Anne's thought it over, she'll change her mind.'

'Aunt Anne loves this cottage, Edmund. It's her true home. I can understand her being afraid of losing it,' considered Amy. 'But if the packet's new owner doesn't keep

Pa on, what will he do? He's not a young man anymore, and the sea is all he's ever known.'

Ramsay flatly refused to talk further about buying the Jenet Rae. Aunt Anne was to and fro from Clockmaker's Cottage as usual, and Amy spent every available hour sewing. She was determined to complete the layette before she took leave of absence from Whiteladies Grange and went to York.

Although the daily household routine at Whiteladies was less hectic since Amelia and Laurence Deane's departure, the atmosphere was unusually lively and gay. Miss Sophie smiled and floated about the house on clouds, anticipating the formal announcement of her engagement and, for her part, Amy was constantly aware of Gilbert's presence.

She caught herself hoping for a glimpse of him, listening for the deep tenor of his quiet voice, and occasionally felt the flutter of butterflies in her tummy if he entered the room where she was working.

Choir practice and Sundays at All Hallows became the happiest times of the whole week, and it pleased Amy that Gilbert frequently sought out her ideas and opinions upon the plans for the harvest festival.

She was eagerly looking forward to their excursion to see the play, and when the day finally arrived, Amy wished Fanny were there to help her decide what to wear and how to arrange her hair becomingly.

'My word, you're looking bonnie!' exclaimed Ramsay, when Amy came downstairs that evening. She was wearing her deep-green skirt and bodice, with the new lace collar and cuffs that Fanny had made for her last birthday. 'Where are you off to?'

'There's a play on at the assembly rooms,' she explained, her cheeks pink. 'Gilbert's taking me to see it. He says–'

'Gilbert Paslew?' cut in Ramsay, his jaw set. 'You're not stepping out with Paslew's son this night or any other!'

'But he'll be here for me at any minute!'

'He'll have a wasted journey then, won't he?' retorted Ramsay. 'I'll see him when he comes, and I want your word you'll not be meeting him again – at church and White-ladies can't be helped, but otherwise you're to stay away from him.'

Amy stood silent, her spine rigid.

'Well? I'm waiting for your promise.'

Amy bit her lip. 'I can't promise. Gilbert and I are friends.'

'What are you thinking of? Going about with Paslew's son?'

'That he's Alfred Paslew's son has nothing to do with it, Pa! I can't understand why you dislike him so! If only you knew him–'

'It's for your own good,' returned Ramsay firmly. 'There's a line in life, and if you know what's good for you, you don't step over it. Them as do come a cropper.'

'It's not fair!'

'Happen not, but the truth is the likes of them and the likes of us just don't mix, lass,' he said more gently. 'Now, be a good girl and go up and wait in your room until he's been and gone.'

She shook her head miserably. 'I can't do as you ask.'

'I'm not asking,' began Ramsay, his temper sorely tested. 'I expect you to–'

Amy heard the approaching carriage and, turning to the window, saw it drawing up alongside Clockmaker's.

'I'm sorry, Pa–'

Sweeping her cloak about her shoulders, she spun on her heels and was gone from the cottage to meet Gilbert Paslew at the gate.

'You look lovely!' He beamed at her, helping her up into the seat. 'I'm so pleased you said you'd come!'

Amy had never seen a proper play before, and was delighted by the spectacle. The rooms and staircases of a medieval manor house appeared like magic upon the boards of the assembly rooms. Exquisitely costumed characters moved about this imaginary world, scheming and plotting and weaving a tale that held her spellbound until the makeshift curtain fell, and she and Gilbert were filing out with the rest of the audience into the cool night air.

'It was wonderful!' she exclaimed. 'Every moment of it!'

During the drive from town, they discussed the play in detail; their conversation eventually moving on to harvest festival, Sophie's forthcoming marriage and somehow, to Amy's embroidery of the layette.

'It's incredibly beautiful, Amy! I was there when Mother was showing it to Clemmie and Sophie,' Gilbert was saying as the cobbles turned to sandy track and the carriage wheels and horse's hoofs became muffled.

'Herbs and wild flowers were such a clever choice for the design, too. Gwendoline will adore it! I'm really looking forward to being an uncle, although Gwen tells me I'm not to spoil my niece or nephew too much!'

'I might have a niece or nephew myself, soon,' said Amy with a smile. 'I'll doubtless find out when I visit Fanny.'

'I wish you'd let me pay for–'

'No, Gilbert,' she interrupted softly. 'Thank you, but no.'

He shrugged in resignation. 'When are you going?'

'I'm not sure. Things are a bit unsettled at home just now,' she replied. 'Your father's offered to sell mine the Jenet Rae.'

'I didn't know! I wasn't even aware Father intended selling the packet.'

'Well, Pa's to give his answer by the month's end, so I'll probably go to York after that and come home just before he sails on his next trip.'

They felt silent for a while. It was a still, clear night with a scattering of stars, and the rising moon was but a silvery sliver. Tawny owls were flying, their calls resonating from deep within the blackness of Friars Wood. The placid horse walked noiselessly onwards down the winding sandy lane until the shore came into sight. The tide was so far out that the pale beach stretched endlessly before them and disappeared into the darkness.

'I'll miss you when you go away, Amy,' murmured Gilbert despondently. 'I don't suppose you have any use for a helpful and willing guide? I spent my boyhood at school in York, so I know all the places of historic and cultural interest!'

Amy shook her head, her soft brown eyes laughing up at him.

'Thought not...' he began, suddenly catching his breath. Allowing the reins to fall from his hands, he tenderly gathered Amy into his arms, his kiss deepening at the intensity of her response.

Breathless and dizzy when their kiss finally ended, Amy nestled contentedly against him as he held her close while the horse plodded dutifully onwards.

All too quickly, the lights of Clockmaker's Cottage slid into view and she was home. Apprehensive of the reaction awaiting her, she was determined Gilbert should not sense her unease.

'I'll see you tomorrow,' he whispered.

A great many possibilities were coursing through Amy's mind as she pushed open the door to her home. However, she was quite unprepared to find Pa and Aunt Anne sitting together at the fireside.

Immediately, she saw her father's angry frown but, even as he was drawing breath, Aunt Anne was greeting her cheerfully.

'Did you enjoy the play?' She smiled at her niece. 'Gilbert mentioned you were both going to see it– He has such a fine appreciation of literature! I came here this evening to speak to your father,' she went on, 'and I stayed to see you because I wanted to tell you myself – I've agreed to Clockmaker's Cottage standing for your father's loan. No, dear–' she raised a hand, silencing Amy's exclamation. 'There's nothing more to be said. It's done.'

Then she put on her bonnet and cloak and swept out of the house.

Hours later, Amy was sitting on the oak chest in her bedroom with her feet tucked under her, gazing from the window, when Edmund appeared in the open doorway.

'May I come in?' he asked.

Tiptoeing past Vicky, who was sleeping soundly with her ragdoll tucked up next to her, he sat beside Amy on the chest.

'What do you make of it all?'

'I'm surprised,' she admitted, her chin cupped in her hand.

Truth to tell, she'd scarcely given a thought to the packet and her father's commitment to buying the boat. Since coming upstairs, her thoughts had all been of Gilbert.

Edmund followed her gaze from the window to the lampblack sky. 'If the packet doesn't make enough money and we lose Clockmaker's Cottage, what'll become of us?'

'We'll manage, Edmund,' she replied with an optimism she scarcely felt. 'We'll manage, because we must.'

Terrible News

'We'll definitely be ready to sail on time!' Ramsay MacFarlane said enthusiastically when Amy and Vicky took his dinner to him aboard the Jenet Rae. 'We're not about to be late – not our first trip under new owner-ship!'

The vessel was alive with noise and activity as the crew and a handful of local men strove to make good whatever repairs money and time allowed. The damp air was pungent with bubbling tar pots, wet hemp and fresh-sawn timbers.

Amy marvelled at the change in her father since he'd become owner of the Jenet Rae. There was a new vigour in his step, and a pride and self-esteem that she had not seen before. The packet just had to succeed! Not only because they would lose their home if it did not but because, watching him now, Amy realised that if the venture failed, then her father's brave heart and spirit would be broken forever.

The following Sunday was harvest festival at All Hallows.

Gilbert, Edmund, Collie Barraclough and his sons had spent most of the previous day driving carts around Monks Quay, collecting everything from cheese to rush-lights, and taking these gifts to the church in readiness for distribution amongst the poor and needy.

Amy and Vicky had joined the womenfolk decorating the pews, pulpit, window ledges and altar with sheaves of oats, barley, wheat and hedgerow fruits.

The congregation on that crisp autumnal morning was swelled by people who were not regular churchgoers, and when Amy saw Dan Ainsworth arriving with his parents and younger brothers, she felt a pang of regret at the loss of his friendship.

As if sensing her gaze, he glanced across to the choir stalls and met her eyes for a moment before turning away and taking his seat.

Reverend Linley's simple sermon of thanks and compassion was well-received by his parishioners, and Gilbert's choice of music and hymns was a resounding success.

The rest of Amy's day was taken up, first with Sunday School, then with helping Reverend and Mrs Linley pack the baskets, and finally with lending Gilbert a hand delivering the harvest bounty all around the parish. It wasn't until the sun was setting and the sky was streaked with vivid paint-box hues that the last basket was delivered and Amy and Gilbert were at last alone, strolling back across the meadows to All Hallows.

'I suppose it's still a little early to descend upon Uncle William and Aunt Lucy,' remarked Gilbert. The vicar and his wife had invited them both for supper, but neither one was in any hurry to relinquish these precious moments.

'I'm happy just strolling and watching the sunset.' Amy sighed contentedly. 'It's been such a good day!'

'A worthwhile sort of day,' agreed Gilbert, lifting her on to the sun-warmed stones of the churchyard wall and then climbing up beside her. All Hallows was built on high ground, and from their vantage point, the country rolled away, either inland to woods and hills, or down to the shore and distant sea, the glittering water aflame with the colours of the setting sun.

'I can't help thinking... Oh, I don't know!' he went on edgily. 'Today I felt really alive! I was doing something useful. Something important. Mostly, days pass by and I haven't done anything of value at all.'

'That's not true! You're helping your father run your family's business, that's important!'

'Is it?' He held her gaze. 'I find it increasingly meaningless.'

'It may not be worthwhile in the same way as your uncle's work,' she argued, 'any more than my sewing and cleaning at Whiteladies Grange is as worthwhile as the work Aunt Anne does at the school, but that doesn't make what you and I do less useful!'

'I have so many privileges, I'm ashamed to be dissatisfied,' he said soberly. 'But more and more, I resent the family business and what's expected of me. Is that very selfish?'

'You're not your father, Gilbert. You have to make your own way in life.' She took his hands in both her own. 'Recently, Pa told us he was meant to be a coal miner like the rest of his family, but he longed to go to sea. Eventually he did.'

'I'm sorry your father disapproves of me, Amy. It must make life at home difficult for you.'

'Pa's just set in his ways. And it isn't really you – not you personally,' she answered frankly. 'Besides, I think he might be getting used to the notion of our being friends.'

'More than friends, I think!' Raising her hand to his lips, Gilbert touched each fingertip with a kiss. 'All the same I don't want to cause any discord.'

'You're not!' She reached up to kiss his cheek before resting her head against his shoulder. 'I'm looking forward to seeing Fanny again, but I wish I wasn't going away to York tomorrow!'

'I don't suppose it would be wise for me to come along and see you aboard the coach?'

'Not really.' She smiled ruefully.

'We could start saying our goodbyes tonight...?' he suggested, gazing down into her wide, brown eyes.

'That seems sensible,' Amy responded, tilting her face to his. 'But we mustn't forget supper at the rectory...'

Although she was already missing Gilbert, Amy's spirits were high during the long, uncomfortable journey from Monks Quay to York.

She was longing to see her sister again. There'd be so much to talk about and catch up with, especially now that Fanny was certain she was expecting. And, of course, Amy had news of her own. She couldn't wait to pour out all her innermost thoughts and feelings about Gilbert.

Nicholas Buxton was waiting patiently for her in York when the weary horses clattered up the cobbled Shambles and towards the coaching inn, The Eagle and Child.

Amy's first question was after Fanny's health.

'She's feeling a little better, I think,' he replied, taking Amy's portmanteau from the coachman. 'At least, she tells me so.'

Nicholas looked anxious and, it seemed to Amy, a good deal older than when she'd last seen him merely months ago. She was immediately concerned. 'What's wrong, Nick? Has something happened to Fanny? Or – or – is it the baby–?'

'No! Nothing of that sort, thank goodness,' he instantly reassured her adding, 'However, she is deeply troubled, with just cause, and I am entirely responsible for her distress.'

'You?' exclaimed Amy in disbelief. 'Nick, you must explain what's going on before I see her!'

'Theo is deeply in debt, Amy. I don't know how or why it has happened – he seldom discusses his business affairs with me; I daresay he believes I lack sufficient brains to understand,' related Nicholas bitterly. 'The reversal in fortune seemed to occur almost overnight. We were living comfortably then, suddenly, creditors were pressing to have their bills settled, tradesmen refused to supply the cook, and lawyers' clerks were hammering at the front door of Carteret Square seeking Theo, but he was already gone.'

Amy's heart sank.

'He told us he was going away for a few days in order to collect monies owed to him,' concluded Nicholas. 'That was almost three weeks ago.'

'Have you heard from him? Do you know where he is?'

Nicholas shook his head. 'I'm so relieved you're here, Amy. I have in mind some steps I might take to ease the financial situation but I haven't wanted to leave Fanny alone.'

'I'm very glad you've stayed with her. She must be desperately worried. But I don't understand why you feel responsible. Theo's debts are not your doing! You can't blame yourself for his imprudence.'

'It's far more than imprudence, and I do blame myself,' he returned harshly. 'I must. I've always been aware that Theo sails close to the wind where money is concerned, but I've never asked for precise details of what he does. Nor questioned his actions.'

'You're not his keeper, Nick.'

'Perhaps I should have been. Last year, when Gilbert asked me to Whiteladies Grange as usual and Theo practically invited himself along, I should've realised he had some scheme in mind.' Taking Amy's arm, he guided her through the busy traffic and crossed Petergate toward the Minster. 'Theo got along really well with Mr Paslew – far better than Gilbert does, actually. I even remember us joking about that, and I do know Mr Paslew has invested a huge amount of money into a company that Theo is involved with. It's something to do with railways. Or at least, it's a company set up to build railways. Except there will never be any railways built – it's all just one great swindle!'

Amy stared at him. She'd heard of gentlemen running up debts, and she'd long believed Theodore to be unscrupulous and dishonest, suspecting him of thieving and worse, but never would she have imagined he'd be behind a fraudulent scheme of this magnitude!

'Just before the wedding, I found out about the swindle,' continued Nicholas. 'I confronted him about it but he refused to change his plans. Theo knew I wouldn't do anything. Knew I was too weak to stand against him!'

'It's not weakness,' Amy put in soberly, recognising too well Nicholas Buxton's dilemma. 'It's family loyalty. And you wanted Theodore to tell Fanny the truth about himself, didn't you?'

Nicholas was too distracted to wonder at Amy's perspicacity. 'I was more concerned for Fanny than for Mr Paslew and the railway shares. I was pretty certain Theo had gilded the lily, and exaggerated his circumstances to Fanny. I didn't think it was fair, and I said so. I didn't want her to be hurt, and now see what my keeping silent has done!'

'We'd all do things differently if we could only go back and change them,' said Amy sensibly, almost gasping at the grandeur of the tall Regency houses lining Carteret Square. 'Everything you've told me, does Fanny know it all?'

'She knows as much as Theo has told her,' he answered. 'Which is to sit tight because he'll sort everything out when he comes home. I'm sorry there wasn't a carriage to meet you, by the way.'

He led the way up eight stone steps to an elegant front door, fitting his key into the brass lock.

'The servants have left, I'm afraid. Even Cook. Apparently, they hadn't been given wages for quite some time.'

He paused, facing Amy squarely.

'I've been so ineffectual in the past, that I don't expect you to believe me when I tell you I won't let any harm come to Fanny. I swear it!'

'I do believe you, Nick,' she murmured, her hand briefly touching his arm. 'Shall we go in?'

Fanny was much thinner than when Amy had last seen her, and her face was pinched and drawn. However, she had lost none of her spark, nor the sharp edge to her tongue.

'I do not wish to discuss Theo,' she said firmly when the sisters were drinking their tea beside the morning-room fire. 'I'm convinced whatever difficulties have arisen will be resolved the instant he returns.'

'Fanny! Theo's been gone three weeks without so much as a word, leaving you to face creditors and–' blurted Amy, instantly wishing she'd bitten back her words. 'I'm sorry. It isn't my business.'

'No, it is not,' retorted Fanny curtly, her blue eyes glittering icily. 'I am in no doubt whatsoever that when my husband comes back to York our life will continue as securely and comfortably as before. Until then, we shall manage as best we can. I'm not always able to get out and about as much as I would choose,' she went on, her mood changing with the subject, 'therefore, I am positively starved of conversation! I want to hear every scrap of news from home but, first of all, you must tell me everything about Gilbert Paslew in minute detail! You're a dark horse, Amy! Stepping out with the son and heir of the richest man in Monks Quay.'

Amy felt hot colour rising to burn her cheeks.

'Well?' persisted Fanny. 'Are you really sweethearts?'

'I'm not sure. It's as you say. I'm me, and he... Well, he's Alfred Paslew's son. But Gilbert is the one for me, Fanny. You once told me I'd know when the right man came along, and I love Gilbert,' answered Amy simply. 'There can never be anyone else.'

The following morning, Nicholas took Amy aside after breakfast. 'Would you mind if I left you and Fanny and went over to Ilkley? I'll be back the day after tomorrow,' he said quietly. 'We have cousins there. The children of Mother's brother. I have it in mind to ask if I might borrow some money. If I'm able, I intend visiting Theo's creditors and trying to reason with them. Perhaps I could keep them at bay until he returns.'

'Of course you must go,' agreed Amy at once. 'Do you think these cousins might be able to help?'

'I'm fairly sure they have the means. You see, when my maternal grandfather died, he left this house and a small legacy in trust for Theo. However, he bequeathed the greater part of his estate to his son, and the property in Ilkley has now passed to my eldest cousin. We've met only once, when I was a boy, but we are family. He might come to our assistance…'

While Nicholas was hastily making ready for his journey, Amy cleared and washed the breakfast dishes. She was checking on the provisions in the huge pantry and deciding upon a light but nourishing meal for later, when Fanny came down into the kitchen and suggested they take a stroll and explore the ancient town together.

The weather was cold but dry, and the sisters had an enjoyable day.

Browsing and window-shopping, they talked and talked of anything and everything, and Amy was left in no doubt that, despite their present financial difficulties, Fanny still loved Theo deeply and had not the slightest suspicion of his ruthless scheming and dishonesty.

The sisters had planned to attend evensong at the Minster, but when they returned to Carteret Square late in the afternoon, Fanny was clearly exhausted and Amy insisted she go upstairs to rest.

After taking her sister a tray of tea, Amy returned to the morning-room and wrote a letter home. At Fanny's behest, she did not mention the problems at Carteret Square.

It was already growing dusk when she set off for the Minster. It was but a short distance away, and she savoured every moment of the crisp, evening air as she walked through the carpet of golden and rusty leaves that were still swirling down all about her from the old trees lining the winding path.

Evensong was an awe-inspiring, breathtaking experience and, as she joined in with the ancient songs of worship, her thoughts strayed again and again to Gilbert and how very much she loved him.

It was quite dark when the service ended and Amy returned to Carteret Square. She prepared a light but sustaining supper for herself and Fanny, and after they had eaten and her sister had retired early to bed, Amy took her sewing into the morning-room and settled to her work.

Lost in concentration upon her embroidery and her thoughts, it was very late before she noticed the hour and rose from the fireside.

With the lamp held high, she walked along the dark, unfamiliar hallway and was about to climb the staircase, when she smelled smoke. It was not chimney smoke, nor from the range, yet it seemed to come from the kitchen.

Quickening her step, she strode down the hall and pushed open the kitchen door. Instantly, she was aware of somebody there in the darkness.

'Who are you?' she demanded loudly, her hand trembling slightly as she raised the light to better illuminate the large room. 'Who is it – *you!*'

'None other.' Rory drew on a cheroot, exhaling a plume of pungent smoke. He was sitting, leaning back in a comfortable chair, his legs stretched out and propped up before him on the scrubbed table. 'I'm waiting to see Buxton. When do you expect him back?'

Recovering her composure, Amy moved into the room and roughly pushed his boots from the table. For all his cockiness of attitude, now that the light shone full upon him, she could see her brother was grimy and dishevelled. He looked exhausted, and surely that was blood staining his shirtfront and coat?

'I don't know whether Theodore will be returning to York at all!'

Rory swore under his breath, wincing as he reached for the grog bottle standing before him on the table.

'How long is he gone?'

'Almost a month.' She looked at the kitchen door. It did not appear damaged in any way. Nor was the small window beside it broken. 'How did you get in? Have you a key?'

'Hardly! Buxton warned me never to come here, but needs must.'

He swilled down a mouthful of liquor. 'Where's the other one – Nicholas – where's he gone? I saw him rushing off with a bag this morning.'

'You've been watching the house?' she exclaimed.

'Once I was sure there were no servants coming and going any more, and young master Nicholas was out of the way, there was nowt to stop me coming in and making myself at home.'

'Why have you come here, Rory? What do you want?'

'Enough money to take me far away.'

'You're to be disappointed then, for there isn't a penny piece here,' she replied briskly. 'Theodore has left his wife and household in the direst straits.'

'I'll just have to rely on you to help me in that case.' He grinned, adding slyly, 'Of course, I could go upstairs and have a word with Fanny. Does she still believe that husband of hers is a saint? I'm sure she'd be interested to hear all about his activities – and only too glad to pay me to keep quiet and go away!'

'You really are despicable!' Amy could not conceal her disgust. 'Fanny is unwell and worried sick besides, yet you'd destroy her just to have your own way!'

'Listen to me, Amy, and listen good! I can't afford to patty-foot around.'

He leapt to his feet, confronting her. Even the spasm of pain creasing his face did not lessen the menace exuding from him. Involuntarily, Amy took a step back.

'Aye, you might well be wary! I'm a

wanted man. And if I get caught, I swear that before I dance at the end of the rope, I'll shop Theodore Buxton and take him with me. So, if you don't want to make Fanny a widow and her unborn babe a fatherless orphan, you'll do exactly what I tell you!'

Amy's legs felt weak at the knees, and she gripped the table edge to steady herself.

'What have you done?'

'Does it matter?'

'What have you done?' she repeated, indicating his bloodstained shirt and coat. 'How were you wounded?'

'I was delivering some goods, if you must know. The bloke baulked at paying what he owed. We had a tussle and he got me with his blade. I laid into him. He went down hard on the cobbles. Didn't get up.'

'You killed a man?'

'I don't know. If I did, I didn't mean to. It was an accident.'

Rory met her gaze, and Amy saw stark fear in her brother's narrowed eyes.

'People were coming and I had to get away. Didn't have time to take the money or anything. I just ran for it.'

Amy stared at him.

'From outward appearances, you and

Theodore Buxton are as different as two men might be; however, beneath the surface you are alike as two peas in a pod! Both of you survive upon your wits and live by guile and deceit instead of honest labour,' she went on, anger and frustration flaring within her. 'Both of you trample all before you, with neither conscience nor loyalty nor scruple for those who care for you!'

'For all your sermonising, you'll do as I say,' he replied, all trace of fear gone from his countenance. 'Besides, like I told you, it was an accident. I'm innocent.'

'I don't know whether to believe this tale of yours or not. My conscience already troubles me for my part in helping you evade justice in Monks Quay,' she snapped. 'I will help you, Rory, as you knew I would. But know also, it is not because of the liar, thief and – heaven forbid – the murderer I now see before me, but for the dear brother you once were so very long ago. You might have become so again,' finished Amy despairingly, 'if only you had been strong enough to mend your ways and work hard to lead a decent, honest life!'

'Like Pa, you mean? Breaking my back grafting to line another man's pockets?' he retaliated scornfully. 'I'd rather take my chances than end up like him – bowed and broken and still scratching for pennies at the feet of the likes of Alfred Paslew!'

'If you survive a thousand years, you'll never be a tenth of the man Pa is!'

'Maybe.' He got up, pushing the bottle of grog into his pocket and starting past her from the kitchen into the hall.

'Where are you going?'

'Reckon I'll take myself up to one of them nice soft beds upstairs – I've not had a decent sleep in a while.' He grinned down at her alarmed face. 'I'll try not to disturb Fanny. Not yet awhile anyhow. Oh, you won't forget about that money I need, will you?'

'I've told you. There's no money here.'

'There's plenty as might be sold.'

'I can't sell Fanny's household belongings!'

'You'll be surprised at what you can do, little sister! I'll pick out a bagful of stuff and you'll take it to the pop shop. Couldn't be easier,' he said, lighting another smoke from her candle and starting upstairs. 'And remember, the quicker you get the money, the sooner I'll be gone, leaving you and her ladyship in peace…'

Amy had no choice but to do as he'd asked.

On the day of Amy's departure from York, Fanny insisted upon accompanying her and Nicholas to the coaching inn. They walked arm in arm along Petergate, talking nineteen to the dozen. For all her present adversity and delicate condition, Fanny's temperament had lost none of its sharpness and spice.

'My blood still boils whenever I think of Rory barging into my home – my home – demanding money to get himself out of trouble!' she fumed. 'How dare he! I can never thank you enough for handling it all for me, Amy. Especially the pawnbroker.'

'You've had enough to contend with of late, without getting involved with that,' replied Amy, choosing her next words carefully, for the slightest criticism of Theodore antagonised Fanny. 'Now Nicholas has spoken to some of the creditors, they might not be so troublesome.'

'And there is no cause for you to mention my present plight to the family,' Fanny declared as the sisters hugged goodbye. 'All will be set to rights soon enough when Theo comes home.'

Heartbreak For Amy

A north-easterly wind had whipped the tide into deep, spume-flecked furrows on the grey wintry morning that Ramsay Mac-Farlane had set sail on his first voyage as skipper and owner of the Jenet Rae.

The packet had been heavily laden, and Ramsay had planned a longer, more ambitious trip than usual.

As the days became shorter and the weeks slipped by, Amy imagined her father's journey and often wondered where exactly he might be.

She unearthed one of his old charts and she and Vicky plotted his course as best they could. Up to Furness, across to the Isle of Man and on to Ireland, over to Liverpool, and then the little boat would hug the ragged Lancashire coast all the way home to Monks Quay.

Despite winter's tightening grip upon the woods and fields, the weather had not yet taken a serious turn for the worse and there was no reason to suppose he would not be ashore in plenty of time for Christmas.

Amy had made the plum puddings and started her Christmas baking soon after returning from York. It had seemed very lonely making all the festive things without Fanny at her side, and she wondered what sort of Christmas her elder sister would have this year.

At least Fanny's regular letters were now bringing more hopeful news. Her health was greatly improved. Theodore was back, and life at Carteret Square appeared to have settled down into a comfortable routine once more. Nonetheless, reading between the lines, Amy couldn't quell the suspicion that all was far from well with her brother-in-law's financial activities.

'It was very frosty last night and all the stars were really bright,' Vicky was saying, holding the tin tightly while Amy carefully spooned cake mixture into it.

The sisters had spent the morning finishing off the Christmas baking, and this light, festive fruit cake, made from Ma's very own recipe, was always last to be made.

'So the Dog Star will be sparklier than ever, won't it? Pa'll easily see his way home.' And he did say he might be back this week, didn't he?'

'Yes, but you know Pa can never promise, Vicky,' cautioned Amy. 'It hasn't been very windy, lately. And if there isn't enough wind to fill the sails,' she finished, giving Vicky the mixing bowl to scrape out, 'the boat can't sail!'

Once the cake was safely in the oven, Amy took off her apron and made ready to follow the family's Yuletide tradition.

'Vicky and I are off up to St Agnes Falls to make the Christmas wishes,' she said, popping her head into the sitting-room where Edmund was studying. 'Are you coming? We're taking a picnic!'

'I have to finish this Latin paper for when Gilbert comes round tonight.' Edmund grimaced, adding innocently. 'I asked him to stay for supper … you don't mind, do you?'

St Agnes Falls – an ancient spring that tumbled down over mossy stones – lay hidden deep in the heart of Friars Wood. Amy and Vicky could hear its soft whisper and splash a good while before they entered the dell, with its overgrown ivy, holly and pagan mistletoe.

Despite the brilliant sunshine pouring down through the leafless branches of the tall trees, patches of glittering white frost were still crisp in the shady nooks and corners of the Falls.

Holding tightly on to Vicky's hand, Amy gazed all about her in wonder. There was something so very special and magical about this beautiful, tranquil place – especially at this time of year!

The sisters silently cast their Christmas wishes before the sparkling waters of the spring; Amy's wish was always the same, however, this year she'd added special words for Gilbert.

Wrapped up warmly against the cold, she and Vicky found a sunny spot for their picnic of sliced bun loaf and toasted beech-nuts.

Afterwards, while her little sister and her ragdoll were collecting the last of the year's sweet chestnuts, Amy took the opportunity to settle down and write to Fanny, and it was Vicky who first heard the approaching hoofbeats.

'Gilbert!' exclaimed Amy in surprise. 'How did you know we were here?'

'I didn't.' He dismounted, and she immediately sensed his dejection. 'It's so peaceful, I always come here whenever I need to get away to think. I've been working with my father all day – although arguing might be more accurate! I can't imagine how he expects us to work together productively when we can never agree about anything.'

He came to her side, staring deep into the crystal-clear waters of the Falls.

'I wish things were different, Amy. However, my being part of the family business is never going to work. Father and I view things so very differently, and compromise is not a word within his vocabulary,' he replied briskly. 'We get along fairly well – it's only when *Paslew & Son* rears its mercenary head that we're constantly at odds. For my part, I believe there are certain basic principles that must be observed, regardless of the figures on a balance sheet.'

'What will you do?'

'I'm not certain, and that's a huge part of the problem,' He met her eyes despairingly. 'When I was at Oxford, everything seemed so very clear. I had such a sure sense of direction regarding my future... I need to find that certainty again, Amy.'

Alarm shot through her. 'You're not going to leave Monks–'

'*Amy!*'

She and Gilbert were instantly on their feet and running across the dell.

Vicky was sitting amongst the crinkled leaves, nursing her foot and looking very sorry for herself.

'What happened?'

'I climbed up the trunk to get that chestnut.' She pointed to a solitary nut left on an old tree. 'And I slipped!'

'You're supposed to gather chestnuts from the ground, not climb up and pick them!' said Amy, gently feeling the little girl's foot. 'No bones broken! We'll go home and put a cold compress on your ankle so it won't swell too much.'

'You can both ride,' Gilbert said, fetching the bay mare. 'Whiteladies is nearest – we'll be there in no time!'

Vicky was unusually bashful and tongue-tied once she was sitting in the drawing-room at Whiteladies Grange, gazing wide-eyed all around her.

She'd never imagined a room could be so big and filled with so many grand things.

Amy quickly bathed and bound her bruised ankle and, at Gilbert's insistence, a tray of hot chocolate and shortbread was sent for from the kitchen.

'Chocolate and shortbread are essential whenever you fall out of a tree,' he told

Vicky. 'There's no finer remedy – ask any physician!'

The three were finishing off their biscuits, and Amy was explaining her plans for Sunday school for the remaining weeks of Advent, when the drawing-room door swung open and Alfred Paslew stood on the threshold.

'I beg your pardon,' he murmured curtly, his astute gaze taking in the scene, before he turned into the hallway once more and noiselessly closed the door.

Although he had not displayed any disapproval, Amy sensed the unspoken censure.

That evening at Clockmaker's Cottage after supper was over and Gilbert had gone home, she worried lest hers and Vicky's presence in the drawing-room at Whiteladies would provoke yet another row between father and son.

Upon her arrival at Whiteladies Grange next morning, long before first light, Amy was confronted by the cold result of Alfred Paslew's displeasure the instant she scurried into the kitchen.

Gladys Braithwaite turned from the range to face her, pushing a dish of coins across the kitchen table.

'Don't trouble to take off your coat! You've been let go.' The cook pursed her lips. 'I'm to give you your wages till the month's end – and you're lucky to get them, considering!'

Amy stared at Mrs Braithwaite in disbelief. 'I've – I've lost my place?'

'I'm only surprised you got away with it for as long as you did!'

'Got away with–'

'Don't come the innocent, miss! You know full well what I mean! Making up to Mr Gilbert like you have!' she went on. 'Your Fanny did well for herself, marrying a gent and all, and I daresay you thought you'd do the same. You played with fire, my girl, and now you've got your fingers burned good and proper!'

Amy stood, sick to her stomach and too shocked even to defend herself. She wanted to turn on her heel and march away; to refuse to scoop the coins from the dish – but the family needed every penny far too badly for her to have the luxury of pride.

Unable to speak and with tears perilously close, she gathered up her wages and walked straight-backed from the kitchen. Once beyond that door, all she wanted was to get away from Whiteladies Grange as fast as she–

'*Amy! Wait!*' a low voice hissed from the shadows of the backstairs.

Clemmie Paslew stepped into the passageway and hugged her impulsively. 'It's awful, Amy! Just awful! Father shouldn't have done this, it's not fair! Mama is dreadfully upset! So are Sophie and I – and Gilbert will be furious when he finds out!'

Mist was seeping up from the sea and Amy's hair and clothing were shrouded with dampness when she returned to Clockmaker's Cottage. Placing the money into the tea caddy, she sank on to one of the kitchen chairs, still wearing her cloak and bonnet. She'd been fortunate to receive wages from Whiteladies, but even so it–

'What are you doing here?' Edmund clattered down the stairs, dressed ready to go out. 'What's wrong?'

She told him. 'At least the family won't be any worse off, not until the end of the month. After that, well, I just don't know.'

'Pa will be home shortly,' replied Edmund optimistically. 'With the proceeds of his first voyage.'

'He has that huge debt to repay. We need every farthing.' Amy's fingers knotted and unknotted in her lap. 'What am I going to do, Edmund? Wherever will I find another place?'

'The weeks before Christmas are busy everywhere. Someone is bound to need an extra pair of hands,' he replied, adding after a moment's thought. 'Jessups' shop! Mr Jessup is looking for an assistant!'

She nodded dismally. 'I saw the card in Mr Jessup's window advertising the position, but I haven't any experience of working in a shop.'

'You can read and write and do arithmetic,' he persisted. 'You love books and writing letters – you're the ideal stationer's assistant!'

'I was dismissed, Edmund! Dismissed without references! Do you really believe a reputable man like Mr Jessup would trust me to serve in his shop? Monks Quay is a small town, folk are bound to gossip about my losing my place at Whiteladies so suddenly. Without good references, what hope have I of ever securing another post?'

'Perhaps I should apply for the position at Jessups'?' he suggested. 'If I had a proper job, as well as helping out at The Mermaid–'

'No,' Amy said decisively, standing to face him. 'Absolutely not. The hopes of our whole family rest with you and your doing well in life. The scholarship examination is in a couple of months; you mustn't throw away all your hard work now!'

'We'll see,' was Edmund's only reply as he took his coat from the back of the door.

It had been a long, dark day, and the afternoon was already drawing towards dusk when Amy finished pressing Vicky's pinafores and set the heavy irons to cool on the hob. Clockmaker's Cottage was shadowy and silent. Even the tide and the seabirds were subdued and distant.

Amy had kept busy, but she felt restless and distracted. Her mind was weary; ragged with dwelling upon what had occurred and what would become of her now.

She almost cried out for joy when she heard the click of the gate and saw Gilbert striding up the path. She flew into his arms.

'I am so sorry, Amy! It's disgraceful, and utterly unjust!' He held her tightly, pressing his lips to her forehead. 'Are you all right?'

She nodded, drawing comfort from the strength of his embrace.

'Did – did you have a row with your father? About me, I mean?'

'He had neither the grace nor the decency to even mention his actions!' returned Gilbert furiously. 'We breakfasted together, and he said not a word. But for Clemmie finding me at the stables and explaining what Father had done, I wouldn't have known! I confronted him... I still find it difficult to accept that my own father could behave so shamefully.' He distractedly pushed a hand through his damp hair. 'I can't bear to look at him, much less work at his side!'

Shaken by the violence of Gilbert's emotions, the consequences of his words only gradually dawned upon Amy. 'No, Gilbert. You can't do this. Not on my account–'

'It isn't just because of you, Amy,' he said gently, his wrath abating. 'I should have taken this step earlier. I can no longer be party to my father's ruthless ambition nor remain under his roof.'

'You've left Whiteladies? But it's your home!' she exclaimed in horror. 'This is all my fault, isn't it? It's because–'

'It's because my father and I have different values,' he interrupted quietly.

'Where will you go?' She drew him to the warmth of the fireside, taking his wet cloak. 'You – you'd be welcome to stay here for a few days...'

'Thank you, but it wouldn't be wise,' he replied at once. 'I shan't stay at the rectory, either, although I'm sure my aunt and uncle would offer me a bed; I don't wish to create friction between them and Father. He has little enough time for Uncle William as it is. No, I came straight here from Whiteladies and until I've made my plans, I'll put up at The Mermaid Inn.'

'The Mermaid?' she echoed, looking round from putting the tea kettle to boil.

'Would you prefer it if I didn't stay there? I know you and Dan Ainsworth were very close once. I wouldn't want to cause any further difficulties for you, Amy.'

'You won't!' She smiled, fetching cups and saucers. 'Dan and I were old friends from childhood. Even though we don't have much to say to one another these days, he and his family are stood good friends and neighbours of ours.'

'I don't suppose I'll be at The Mermaid for very long, anyway,' he remarked, drawing her on to his lap.

'What are you going to do?' she murmured fearfully, her face close to his. 'Will – will you go back to Oxford?'

'All I'm certain of is that I mean to earn my own living. Since I'm no longer working for my father, I'll not rely upon his wealth either. It's immoral to be a gentleman of leisure when women and children are forced into virtual slavery in mines and mills to avoid starvation. I have to build my own future.' He stared past her to the glowing coals of the fire. 'But first, I must be absolutely sure the direction I'm taking is the true one. Perhaps I should look to your faithful Dog Star for guidance!'

A hoard of terrors visited Amy that night, keeping her from sleep and tormenting her with fears. Fears for Pa somewhere out at sea, for Edmund and Vicky, for the sea-worthiness of the Jenet Rae and the security of their home, and for the bleakness of her own prospects.

Still more dominant during those long hours of wakefulness were Amy's anguished thoughts about Gilbert.

Although he hadn't yet made any decisions, he was going to leave Monks Quay. She was sure of it.

She tossed and turned, exhausted, yet denied rest. She'd understood how shocked and distressed he had been yesterday afternoon, but only now did she realise he'd scarcely mentioned her dismissal from Whiteladies, nor the desperate plight it had brought her to. He'd spoken at length about many things, but not once of Amy, or of the affection and attachment they shared.

In the cold, lonely hours before dawn, she stared wide-eyed into the darkness, agonising over whether the direction and future Gilbert sought included her. Or had she already lost him…

After taking Vicky to school, she gathered a trug of fresh evergreens and went into All Hallows, where she was arranging the glossy greenery when the west door opened to admit Eleanor Paslew, her footsteps soft upon the stone flags.

'Good morning, Amy.' Mrs Paslew smiled hesitantly. 'I was on my way to visit you at Clockmaker's Cottage and saw you coming into the church. However, if you're busy…'

'Not at all, Mrs Paslew!' she replied, returning the smile. 'The Erskines' new baby is being christened this morning. It's such a dreary day, I thought a few evergreens around the font and pews might make it all a bit more cheerful.'

'You're a very thoughtful young woman, Amy. I'm deeply sorry to lose you from Whiteladies Grange. I believe you're aware of the high regard my daughters and I have for you. I hope this might prove useful.'

Extending a gloved hand, the older woman offered a letter addressed, *To Whom*

It May Concern. Inwardly, Amy heaved an enormous sigh of relief. It could only be a reference! And was therefore her assurance of securing employment.

'Thank you, ma'am.'

'It's owed to you, Amy. And I wonder if you might do me a favour? You may recall measuring for new curtains for the drawing and dining-rooms and Mr Paslew's study?'

Amy nodded. 'I wrote out the order and posted it to Mosleys' last week.'

'Would you consider making the curtains for me? Splendid! As soon as the material arrives from Liverpool, I'll have it brought out to you at Clockmaker's Cottage. Meanwhile, if you'd continue doing the regular weekly sewing for Whiteladies I'd be very much obliged.'

Amy's spirits were singing as she swiftly finished arranging the foliage. She'd been given a glowing reference, had regular work sewing for Whiteladies, would have the huge job of making the curtains and, most importantly of all, Eleanor Paslew clearly did not disapprove of Amy's friendship with her son!

Leaving All Hallows, she went to find Gilbert at The Mermaid Inn, taking pains to avoid bumping into Dan. She was aware he still had tender feelings for her, and was anxious not to hurt him more than she had already.

'Are you sure you want to do this immediately?' queried Gilbert, when the pair were striding arm-in-arm down Abbotsgate. 'Right this very minute?'

'Absolutely! Thanks to your mother, I have a wonderful reference and I'm going to ask Mr Jessup if he'll take me on as his assistant!'

'In your present mood, he won't dare refuse!'

They'd reached the stationer's crooked little shop, with its windows filled with books and paint-boxes.

'I'll wait for you in Miss Bower's tearoom.'

But Gilbert was actually waiting on the street outside Jessups' when Amy emerged triumphant.

'I start first thing tomorrow morning!'

'Then we must make the most of today,' he declared, taking her arm. 'Coffee and almond tarts at Miss Bower's to celebrate?'

They were settling into a secluded corner table when the tiny brass bell above the low door jangled violently, and the door itself banged back against its hinges. Ned Yarkin stood in the doorway, framed by the gloom of the afternoon.

'Amy, lass – I've already seen Edmund – said you'd likely be here.' The old man struggled to get his breath. 'I were down on the shore collecting coal. I spotted her with my spyglass – the Jenet Rae–'

He broke off as the bells of All Hallows commenced tolling, and Amy's blood was ice-water in her veins. She grasped the elderly man's trembling hands.

'She's in trouble, lass–'

With the melancholy peal of the bells loud in her ears, Amy raced down the cobbled streets from the town to the shore, heedless of Gilbert bidding her to wait while he fetched horses. Other folk were running, too, alerted by the church bells to a peril on the sea.

It was a dull day and the darkest time of year, and the already poor light was fading fast when Amy reached the hard, damp sand. She strained her eyes to peer into the grey murkiness but could see nothing.

'Perhaps Mr Yarkin was mistaken,' suggested Gilbert.

'I've been praying that be true, but if Ned Yarkin says it is so, then it is,' she answered. 'Before he became potman at The Mermaid, Ned Yarkin sailed the seas for sixty years and more. He wouldn't make a mistake about a vessel in distress – there! There she is!'

An indistinct grey blur pitched and rolled against a grey sky and even greyer sea.

'Here, lass–' Ned pushed the spyglass into her cold hands. 'Take a look– Ah! Here comes Edmund!'

Amy turned to see her brother arriving on the shore along with Dan Ainsworth and *his* brothers. There must have been a score or more other people besides them; men, women and children clustered in tight little groups, watching the drama unfolding before them.

'Is she going to do down?' Amy's question was directed at Ned.

'What is it that's gone wrong?' put in Gilbert, also to the elderly man.

'Wind's wrong, and there's not tide enough to bring her in,' considered Ned, squinting out across the rise and fall of slate-grey water, now punctured by a ramrod straight barrage of rain. 'Your pa's only chance is to bring her through the gulley to the pool, then to drop anchor and bide his time. He'll have to be quick about it, though,' finished the old man morosely. 'Or the ebb'll take him straight on to Judas Rock and the packet'll go the way of many another boat before her!'

'What's happening, Mr Yarkin?' asked Edmund desperately. 'What's the gulley and pool? Is Pa doing what you said?'

'He doesn't seem to be doing anything. She's not making any way,' he muttered, taking back the spyglass and focussing upon the tiny vessel. 'The gulley's hard to find at best, and from that distance in this light, your pa'll scarce be able to see shore at all. You lads–' Ned turned to those standing around the shore and, suddenly, the old pot-man who was the butt of many a joke, had every man's undivided attention. 'Half of you go up to Fiddler's Pike and the rest out to Smedley's Mill. Take torches, anything you can get that'll keep alight in this wet. And make sure you do keep 'em alight – the lives of every man aboard that boat are depending on you!'

'Edmund's going to Fiddler's Pike, and I'll head up to the mill,' murmured Gilbert, his arm protectively about Amy's shoulders. 'Unless you'd rather I stayed? I really don't like to leave you alone.'

'I'll be all right. Mr Yarkin's here,' she whispered brokenly. 'I only wish I could do something, instead of standing here watching and waiting!'

Hugging her tightly, he went from her side and disappeared amongst the throng of men and boys streaming with all speed back up to the town.

'Do ye know about the gulley, lass?' asked Ned, when they were left alone. 'No? It's a stretch of water that leads between the sandbanks into a deep pool that's safe anchorage whatever the tide. Three fathoms it is, even at low water. Once your pa gets there, he'll be safe as houses.'

Amy wasn't cold, but she couldn't stop shivering.

'Why have the men gone out with torches?'

'Ah, the pool isn't buoyed! When you're out at sea, the only sure guide is to line up two landmarks – Fiddler's Pike and Smedley's Mill, which is lower down. If you stick to that line – and it's a tight one – you can sail nice and easy between the seaward sandbank and the landward sandbank, straight into the pool's deep water. But in this dusk and with the rain and all, Ramsay won't be able to see the landmarks from his boat. Torches will light them up grand and your pa will spot them no trouble!'

'Like beacons?' she said through chattering teeth. 'I understand now, thank you – for everything, Mr Yarkin.'

The old man stood with her for a while longer before shuffling away, and Amy absently heard him talking to Dan, who'd brought down the waggon.

She half-turned, and caught the exchange of a glance between the two men that filled her with dread.

Despite Ned's encouraging talk, was the Jenet Rae already a lost cause?

Presently, Dan came over to where she was standing. 'Here, wrap yourself up in this oilskin,' he murmured, draping the garment about her. 'Is there anything you want me to do, Amy?'

She met his concerned eyes and shook her head. But he waited with her, nonetheless, and they both saw the procession of torches moving along to Smedley's Mill and snaking upwards to Fiddler's Pike.

'Here she comes!' Ned Yarkin's shout went up. He passed his spyglass to Amy. 'Your pa's seen the torches and he's taking her through the gulley!'

Amy held the glass to her eye, hardly able to watch, yet unable to tear her eyes from the boat inching its way through perilous waters.

'He's taking it steady … that's good,' muttered Ned, more to himself than anyone else. 'Ramsay'll be watching the torches and keeping his eye on the water below at the same time.'

It was nearly dark. The wind was freshening. Amy's gaze was fixed upon the Jenet Rae. She heard Dan's exclamation.

'Ned – the torches!'

She raised her face, following their gaze. The lights on Fiddler's Pike were guttering, all but extinguished by the sheeting rain.

'Let's hope the lads get 'em going again quick-smart,' said Ned, raising the spyglass again and looked out to sea. 'I reckon there's not much farther to the pool and – *she's drifting off-course!*'

Amy snatched the glass but, seeing nothing, handed it back to Ned, unable to speak. One glance was all the old seaman needed. Amy heard his shuddering breath.

'She's gone – run aground on the landward bank!'

The stillness and tension exploded into noise and activity.

Ned was yelling orders and folk were running in all directions.

'Amy! Amy! Listen to me!' Dan shook her hard, jolting her back from shock. 'Ned says the waves are not running high nor strong enough to break her up. We're putting out rowing boats and we'll bring your da and the crew ashore. Why don't you go home to your aunt and Vicky? There's nothing you can do here.'

She shook her head.

'Have it your own way. Stay close to Ned. I'm fetching down the boat now. Da and me'll row out as soon as we're able.'

'Dan!' Finding her voice at last, Amy clutched both his hands. 'Please be careful!'

He stood stock-still, and Amy recognised the emotion behind his eyes.

Then he touched a hand to her cold cheek and sprinted up the shore towards the boat-house.

It was completely dark when Dan and his father pushed their rowing boat out into the lapping black water, the only light being that from the spitting torches still burning at the two landmarks. Scrabbling aboard when she was afloat, they lit their lantern and took the oars, pulling hard to make headway.

Three other boats followed their lead.

From the shore, all that could be seen out to sea was the flickering of the lanterns like so many darting fireflies in the void of night.

And soon, even they disappeared and there was just darkness and the soft rush and whisper of the distant sea.

At long last, pinpoints of lantern-light appeared again.

'Coming ashore!' The call was barely audible through the rain but loud enough for those waiting to wade into the shallows, ready to grab the rowboats when they drew near, and haul them on to the safety of the shore.

Collie Barraclough's sons were first, their boat dragged clear of the water by onlookers. One glance told Amy that Pa was not among the three men rescued. The next boat was empty, save for the rowers. The last two came in together, Jim Erskine sat doubled up on the one, and a cry escaped Amy's lips when she saw only Dan and his father aboard the other.

'Take it easy, lass!' Dan leapt over the side and caught her as she floundered through the shallows, peering down into the boat. 'He's passed out. His leg's hurt, but he's all right!'

Ramsay lay white and still, his leg bloody and torn. Amy watched Dan and his father lift him from the boat and put him carefully into the waggon.

223

'We nearly made it, Miss MacFarlane,' said one of the packet's crewmen as he passed. 'A right shame, it was. The sandbank got us right at the end.'

'I'm glad you're safe,' she managed to say. 'What about Jim Erskine?'

'Bad, miss. I don't know what happened, but he's in a right mess!'

'There'll be food and a few tots at The Mermaid!' Dan called to the crewman, whose name Amy didn't know. 'Oh, and...'

Dan moved out of her hearing and she leaned into the waggon bundling the blankets closer around her father. She started when Gilbert suddenly appeared beside her, with Edmund just a short distance behind.

'Ned told me they got all the crew off,' he began earnestly. 'You must–'

'This is your father's fault.' She glared at him, her fingers gripping the edge of the wagon. 'He'd neglected the packet. Hadn't repaired her. The Jenet Rae was barely seaworthy when your father sold her to mine. And because Pa isn't rich, he risked his life on a voyage just to pay his way and provide for his family! But for Ned, Pa and the crew could've died tonight! Do you realise that, Gilbert? Pa might've drowned, and it would've been your family's fault!'

'Amy, we need to get your da home.' Dan strode across to the waggon and swung up on to the seat next to Edmund. 'There's no time to hang about!'

Grasping the hand Dan extended, she clambered up beside him, leaving Gilbert standing alone as the waggon pulled away towards Clockmaker's Cottage.

Hours later, when Ramsay was sleeping easily on the bed that Amy had made up for him in the sitting-room, she tiptoed out into the kitchen.

Edmund looked worn out, but he sat at the table still, his head bowed over his books.

'You should be in bed – not studying!'

'Couldn't sleep,' he replied. 'I can't concentrate on this, either, but it's better than thinking about what might have happened to Pa and the crew.'

'Oh, Edmund.' She sat across from him, burying her face in her hands. 'I thought we'd lost him!'

'I heard Mr Ainsworth saying the packet would've been swept on to Judas Rocks and been smashed to matchwood but for Ned Yarkin,' murmured Edmund soberly. 'Folk laugh at him at The Mermaid, and think he's a crotchery old-and-so, but Mr Yarkin saved them all, didn't he?'

'Yes, he did. We've a lot to be thankful for this night.' She sighed. 'Pa's leg will heal with time, but Doctor Tadman said Jim Erskine might lose his arm. It was badly crushed when the packet ran aground. His baby was christened today. What sort of Christmas will that family have? How will they manage, if Jim is crippled for life?'

Edmund studied her pinched face before speaking. 'What you said to Gilbert about the Jenet Rae … it might've been true but it wasn't his fault, Amy. None of this is.'

'You're right,' she admitted unhappily. 'I don't know what came over me. I was so angry and frightened. I still feel frightened, and I don't even know why. Pa's safe and it's all over, yet I still have this … this awful fear inside me and it isn't going away. I want to cry all the time.'

'You need to get some sleep. When you see Gilbert again, everything will be all right. He'll have understood. You'll see.' Edmund tried to reassure her. 'Go on up to bed. I'll sit with Pa in case he wakes.'

'Edmund tells me you're starting a new job today,' remarked Ramsay, when Amy took his breakfast into the sitting-room. 'I never cared much for you skivvying for the likes of them up at Whiteladies Grange, but selling books and suchlike at Jessups' is a big step up in the world.'

'Mrs Paslew did give me a very good reference, and she's sending sewing for me to do here at home.'

'Eleanor Paslew's a decent enough woman. Your aunt thinks highly of her. Shouldn't you be getting along to your new job?'

'Not today, Pa!'

'Why not? Because of me? I may have a gammy leg, but I'm not a helpless invalid!' he retorted. 'Nay, lass. You go off to Jessups'. I'll be glad of some time to myself. I've a deal of thinking to do.'

During Amy's first days working at the stationer's, there were so many new things for her to learn and remember. She had to concentrate so hard upon her varied duties that there wasn't time to dwell upon the family's troubles. Nor her harsh words to Gilbert. She hadn't seen or heard from him since the Jenet Rae ran aground and he and Edmund had taken to meeting at the schoolhouse for their study sessions.

How swiftly everything had changed! Just one week ago, she'd felt such great happiness and contentment whenever she and Gilbert were together and she'd dream of their being together always. Then that afternoon at St Agnes Falls, he'd spoken about returning to Oxford and Amy's dreams had been shot through with doubts.

Had Gilbert ever loved her, really loved her? She fretted as she walked from Jessups' towards Clockmaker's Cottage. Or did he merely care for her, as she did for Dan Ainsworth? Was this pain and sadness inside her how Dan had felt? Was this aching emptiness how it felt to love somebody completely and not have that love returned? She bowed her head against the sea wind and quickened her step home.

The Ainsworths' waggon was drawn into the sheltered side of the cottage, and when Amy went indoors she found Dan, Ned Yarkin and Edmund gathered in the sitting-room with her father. Pa was in his favourite armchair, his leg propped on a stool and a sturdy stick at his side.

'Ned and Dan went out to the Jenet Rae the day after she foundered, saved what cargo they could and got the money for it,' explained Ramsay with a broad grin. 'Ned reckons, although the boat took a beating, she's not beyond repair and once she's patched up, she should fetch a bob of two!'

'That's wonderful, Pa!' She looked from Ned to Dan. 'Thank you both, you've – excuse me, I'll just see who's at the door!'

'Could be Collie Barraclough and Da!' called Dan after her. 'They said they'd follow us up…'

However, when Amy opened the front door, it wasn't Collie Barraclough and Mr Ainsworth standing before her, but Gilbert.

'Hello, Amy.' He spoke diffidently, not moving towards her. 'I came to ask after your father. And yourself.'

'He's on the mend,' she mumbled uncomfortably. 'Thank you.'

'And yourself?' he repeated. 'I've been concerned, but I didn't want to… I thought it might perhaps be best to wait a while… I was up to Jessups' this evening, in the hope of meeting you when you left the shop, but you'd already gone.'

'Mr Jessup has been very kind, letting me leave a little early each evening.' She raised her eyes, meeting his gaze steadily. 'Gilbert, I'm so very sorry for what I said on the shore. I–'

'That terrible night is all over, Amy,' he gently interrupted. 'Have you heard about Jim Erskine? Dr Tadman managed to save his arm.'

'Thank goodness! Have you seen Jim yourself?'

'Yes, my uncle and I visited his family earlier today. The other three crewmen are doing well, too. It was Jim and your father who were most badly hurt.' He glanced at the waggon standing beside the cottage. 'You have visitors. This obviously isn't a convenient time, but I need to talk to you about my plans. Can we meet later this evening? Or tomorrow, perhaps–'

He reached for her hand but Amy jerked back, pulling free as though burned.

'I – I don't...' She was flustered, shocked at the flame of emotion his touch provoked. Her heart was hammering, hot colour flooding her face. She read the rejection and confusion in Gilbert's clear eyes, yet could only stare wordlessly at him. She just wanted to take him into her arms.

'Amy!' Dan emerged from the sitting-room into the unlit kitchen behind her. 'Are you coming back in?'

'Yes, I'm coming,' she answered without turning around. She was gazing up into Gilbert's face, and what she saw there overwhelmed her with longing and with loss. He didn't love her. He was going to leave her.

That's what he'd come to tell her – and she knew she couldn't bear to hear him say it. She swallowed hard, lowering her eyes. 'I'd better go in. People are waiting.'

'Yes, I can see that,' he returned coldly. 'I just wanted you to know I'm going to Oxford.'

'When,' she heard herself ask.

'On the next coach.'

'How long will you be away?'

'I'm not yet certain.'

'You won't leave Monks Quay for good?'

She lifted her eyes, only to flinch from his hostile expression.

'There isn't any reason for me to stay.' He turned away down the path, pausing with his hand on the gate to look back at her. 'Goodbye, Amy.'

A silent cry choked her throat. She took in a deep breath, fighting the wild impulse to run after him and beg him not to go. Instead, she stood shivering on the doorstep. Tears of grief blinding her as she watched him mount his horse and ride away without a backward glance. Then Dan was beside her once more. She followed him into the kitchen and lit the lamps.

The Dog Star

Amy missed him most of all on Sundays. She missed hearing his voice singing in the choir stalls just a few feet behind her; seeing him come into All Hallows when the children had gone home and she was tidying up after Sunday school; strolling home across the meadows with him or having supper together at the rectory.

Reverend and Mrs Linley still welcomed her into their home. However, it wasn't the same without Gilbert and she found herself making excuses and declining their invitations. Being there in the rectory with the elderly, happily married couple, reminded Amy too sharply of what might have been, if her love for Gilbert had been requited.

At this time of year especially, with the church and town decked for Christmas, Amy felt Gilbert's absence constantly.

After finishing at Jessups' that evening, she set off along Abbotsgate to the greengrocer, in search of small oranges for Sunday's Christingle. Having made her purchases, she was weaving her way along the busy street when Dan Ainsworth caught up with her.

'I'll walk you home – market days are even more boisterous than usual leading up to Christmas!'

'I'd noticed!' She grimaced, skirting around a chestnut seller who was plainly the worse for wear and loudly heckling the pieman on the opposite corner.

'Edmund told me you'd offered him free board and lodgings at The Mermaid. It's good of you, Dan. Thanks.'

'Edmund's a good lad and a hard worker, and it'll only be the room above the stable.' Dan shrugged. 'But it might tide him over until you get settled somewhere. Have you been told when you have to leave Clock-maker's?'

'Not until after Christmas, that's all we know as yet. Apparently, the banker who lent Pa the money will send us a notice to quit, telling us the date on which we need to leave the cottage.'

'It's a rum do and no mistake,' he said sympathetically. 'Ned and me and all of us, we've been keeping our eyes open for a place that might suit you.'

'Well, there's an empty cottage in the

middle of Fisherman's Terrace, but it's not much more than a hovel. Aunt Anne's insisting we move in with her. However, the schoolhouse is so tiny, it'd be awfully cramped. Until Pa finds another job, we won't know how much rent we can afford, but he's determined we'll find a new home long before we're evicted from Clockmaker's,' she concluded soberly. 'He couldn't bear the shame of that.'

'Your da's a proud man. His dignity's already taken a battering with losing the Jenet Rae.'

'It's not being the family breadwinner any more that's really eating away at him.' She frowned. 'He started looking for work as soon as he was up and about and able to walk, but Pa's not a young man. Jobs aren't easy to find.'

'Is it right he's not going back to sea?'

She nodded. 'It surprised us, too. Pa's willing to try his hand at anything other than going cap in hand to Alfred Paslew to ask for a job at the clay pits.'

'I don't blame him.' Dan paused. 'Which way are you going?'

'I'm taking these oranges to All Hallows for the Christingle.' She laughed out loud at his puzzled expression. 'You should come to church more often, Dan Ainsworth!'

'I'll be there on Christmas Day, just like every year!' he declared, walking with her. 'Amy, have you heard from Fanny lately? Do you know what Theodore Buxton is up to these days?'

She gave him a wry glance. 'He's still in York. According to Fanny, he doesn't go away as often as he used to and he's planning a very lavish festive season. They've taken on new staff, arranged dinners and parties and employed a nurse to look after Fanny and the baby when it comes. Why do you ask?'

'I've told you about Sam Tristram, haven't I? Editor of *The Lancashire Clarion?* How he asked me to write up any local stories and send them in? Well, Sam's heard a rumour about a big railway shares swindle. Alfred Paslew was one of the investors.'

Amy's eyes widened. 'That's what Nick spoke about! Theo's been selling shares in a railway that's never going to be built!'

'Happen Buxton's chickens are on their way home to roost,' returned Dan with a smile. 'Sam Tristram's asked me to see what I can find out. I'm going up to Whiteladies to see if Paslew'll give me his comments for *The Clarion* – he'll probably send me packing with a flea in my ear! His sort don't like being made a fool of, nor want it written about for all to read.'

'Is that what it was? Foolishness?'

'He's been conned, hasn't he?' remarked Dan. 'Duped by a smooth-talking swindler. Mind, Paslew's not the only one who was taken in. A lot of rich men invested, and some'll be ruined.'

'What about Alfred Paslew? Will he be ruined?'

'Paslew's not that much of a fool!' Dan snorted derisively. 'No, his sort always cover their backs. He'll probably just cut his men's wages to make up his losses.'

They passed through the lychgate and walked up to All Hallows. With a deep sigh, Amy pushed open the west door and, lighting the candle, walked into the dark church.

'Amy, do you remember me saying I'd keep asking you until you said yes? Well, I'll not ask you again. I know now there's no point. It's him, isn't it? Gilbert Paslew.' Dan paused. 'Do you write to each other?'

She shook her head. 'But he corresponds with Edmund.'

'So, Gilbert Paslew's gone, and you don't hear from him. He might never come back, lass. And just because I'll not ask you, it

236

doesn't mean my feelings have changed. They haven't, and this seems the place to tell you so. All you need do is say the word, Amy.'

He watched the candlelight flickering across her huge, sad eyes.

'And if you ever say "yes", I'll have you walking up this aisle so fast it'll make your head spin!'

The winter's first dusting of powdery snow helped the runners of Edmund's sled move easily across the coarse grass and fallen leaves in Friars Wood. He and Amy were gathering firewood, tying it into bundles and loading it upon the sled, while Vicky had gone in search of the perfect Yule log for Clockmaker's Cottage.

'It's queer to think this'll be our last Christmas at Clockmaker's, isn't it?' said Edmund, tying off another bundle. 'I hope Pa finds a job soon. He doesn't speak of it, but he goes to the boatyard every morning in case they need extra hands. Then he waits around at the quayside to be hired for a day's work. But they always pick the young men.'

'I had no idea!' cried Amy. 'Poor, poor Pa! After being a skipper for all these years! It must be so humiliating for him. I wish we could have spared him that.'

Leaving Edmund to stack the last of the firewood on to the sled, Amy wandered through the trees into the dell and sank to her knees before St Agnes Falls. A few minutes passed and she sensed, rather than heard, Edmund joining her.

'I wonder where we'll be this time next year?'

'You'll be away at school,' she replied lightly, 'having passed the scholarship examination with flying colours!'

'I'm starting to really believe I will, you know,' he said seriously. 'Gilbert's an excellent teacher. I never would have reached this standard without his help.'

'Is – is Gilbert well?'

'Mmm. He always asks after you and the family.'

'We parted so … suddenly. It wasn't even a proper goodbye. Will he be at Whiteladies for Christmas?'

Edmund shook his head. 'He's staying with the family of one of his old tutors in Oxford. The Right Reverend someone-or-other. Gilbert's intending to offer himself as a candidate for holy orders.'

Amy smiled wistfully, touching her fingers

to the spring's cold, clear waters.

'Perhaps the Dog Star showed Gilbert his rightful path after all!'

'What?' queried Edmund.

'Nothing!' she replied, rising and brushing down her skirt. 'Let's see if Vicky has found us a Yule log.'

The three emerged from Friars Wood with their laden sled and headed down Lane End towards the schoolhouse, to leave Anne's share of the firewood.

'Aunt Anne must have company!' remarked Edmund, when the school came within sight. 'In a carriage, no less!'

'That's the Paslew carriage! We'd better wait a bit. We don't want to barge in,' said Amy, slowing her step. 'Let's go along the riverbank and find some good seed heads to decorate the Christmas table.'

Edmund stowed the sled just inside the little north gate of All Hallows and they set off along Lane End. A stout man carrying a small black bag was hammering on the door of the brick house nearest the river.

'I think that's Meggie Huxley's dad,' muttered Edmund, who'd admired Meggie from afar for some time. 'Doesn't look very pleased, does he?'

'Judging from the bag, he must be the

landlord collecting his rents,' said Amy, glancing at the house's grimy windows. 'I don't think he'll have much luck there – it looks empty!'

They'd no sooner passed Mr Huxley when he turned around and called out after them.

'Miss! Do you know anything about the folks who live here? A couple, with three or four bairns. Have you seen them today?'

'I'm sorry, I don't know them,' she replied, looking at the house once more as she and the others continued along the riverbank. When they returned a short while later with a basketful of silvery teasel, the landlord was still working his way along Lane End, collecting rents.

'Aye, the house is empty, miss!' was Huxley's response to Amy's enquiry. 'I've just let myself inside and there's not so much as a stick or a thread! Done a flit, they have. Cleared the place out and gone off owing their rent money!'

Upon finding out how much the rent was, Amy asked if she might view the house and Huxley handed over the key.

'By the time you've looked around, I'll be collecting across the road. You can fetch the key to me there. Don't be long making up your mind about the house, though. I need to get a tenant right away! I can't afford to lose another week's rent money!'

The MacFarlanes stood outside, looking up at the brick house for a few minutes before unlocking the door and going inside.

'Everything needs a thorough scrubbing, but that's easily remedied,' Amy commented, going through the three downstairs rooms. 'Mr Huxley must be a decent landlord, for the house seems in good repair.'

'Come and have a look up here!' called Edmund, adding, when Amy and Vicky had climbed the narrow stair, 'The windows on that side overlook the church, and from here you can see for miles across Friars Wood to the hills.'

'There's the big house!' exclaimed Vicky, pointing to the stone roofs and chimneys of Whiteladies Grange.

'And the garden could be made nice,' commented Amy.

'It's very near the school, too,' remarked Edmund.

'Are we going to live here?' Vicky's bright blue eyes darted excitedly from Edmund to Amy. 'Are we?'

'We'll see what Pa thinks.' Amy smiled and tugged Vicky's plaits as they went downstairs. 'I'll return Mr Huxley's key and then we'll take Aunt Anne her firewood!'

Vicky burst into the schoolhouse and told Anne all about the empty house at Lane End long before Amy and Edmund had put away the firewood and taken off their coats.

'I didn't know the family very well,' remarked Anne, setting down a tray of tea and hot buttered toast. 'They weren't church-goers and they didn't send their children to school – which didn't make me well-disposed towards them – however, I had no inkling they were the sort to sneak away without paying their bills!'

'Providing Pa approves, I think we should take it,' said Amy, swirling honey on to her toast. 'The rent is reasonable and the house seems solid.'

'I remember those houses at Lane End being built when your mother and I were young. They were much admired.' Anne joined them at the table. 'You've only just missed Eleanor Paslew. She came visiting this afternoon and we had such a nice conversation, wandering down Memory Lane for much of the time! Eleanor has invited me to Whiteladies Grange for tea! I shall look forward to it, and she brought me a box of sugared almonds. Even after so many years, she remembered sugared almonds were my favourites. I've put the box away – we'll open it after Christmas dinner.'

'Mrs Paslew always spoke very fondly of you when I was at Whiteladies,' began Amy. 'Did you have a falling out or something?'

'No. Never so much as a cross word passed between us. As we grew up, I suppose our lives went in different directions and we simply drifted apart. Eleanor has it in a nutshell when she said it was so very easy to lose touch with those you care about and not even notice time rushing by,' concluded Anne, and it seemed to Amy her aunt's gaze was fixed sternly upon her. 'If reunions are delayed, all too soon it becomes too late and the parting is forever.'

When Ramsay came home after spending another day searching for work, Amy looked up from her sewing and knew from her father's face he had not been successful.

She saw the grimace of pain as he sat down, easing his right leg out straight in front of him and propping his stick against the table.

He drank the hot, sweet tea she put before him without a word.

'Are you certain about coming ashore?'

she ventured. 'You love the sea, and with all your experience, any master would be glad to have you sign on.'

'It's high time I came ashore and looked after my family,' he replied wearily. 'Should've done it years ago. That truth hit me hard when the Jenet Rae was getting pulled by the ebb up toward Judas Rocks. I kept thinking about the three of you being left to fend for yourselves, and me not being around to watch you grow up. Or see Fanny's babe when it comes. We could've all drowned that night. Probably would've, but for Ned's sending out the torches. So you see, lass, my mind's made up. I don't care what I do – not even if it's Paslew's clay pits, although that will be a last resort – as long as it's honest work and we're all together–'

'Pa!' Vicky barrelled into the cottage after helping Edmund stack the firewood. 'We've found a new house!'

While Ramsay had another cup of tea, they told him about Lane End.

'I know that house, and it's a good stout one.' He drained his tea and got awkwardly to his feet. 'I'll go and see Mr Huxley right away and get my name on the rent book. We'll move in on Boxing Day – I just hope we're in time and nobody else has snapped it up!'

Nobody had. Amy and the others went into Monks Quay with Ramsay, and they walked back to Clockmaker's in good spirits, with a month's rent paid and the rent book and keys of the house in Lane End safely in their possession.

They were about five minutes from the cottage when a figure appeared from the darkness.

'Ah! There you all are!' Dan greeted them. 'I've just been knocking at your door. This letter came on tonight's coach. It's not Fanny's handwriting, but I thought it might be important.'

Dan caught Amy's eye as Ramsay thanked him and took the thick letter.

When the others moved on towards Clock-maker's, Dan motioned to Amy to hang back. He obviously wanted to see her alone.

'What?'

'That letter might be important – it looks like it's travelled a long way – but bringing it out here was an excuse to see you,' he confessed shamelessly. 'We're having a Christmas dance at The Mermaid this market night. Will you come with me? All the money goes to the Parish Fund, so if you refuse, you'll be doing needy folk out of their pennies.'

'Dan, I still love Gilbert,' she told him. 'I always shall.'

'Fair enough. But what's the harm in two old friends spending an evening together?' he persisted brightly. 'It is Christmas!'

'You're hopeless.'

'I'm also a very good dancer – so I'm told. You can't shut yourself away forever,' he went on. 'Will you come?'

She reflected a moment, before nodding. 'I'd like to go dancing with you.'

'Good lass!' He looked sorely tempted to kiss her, but didn't. 'I knew you wouldn't let me end up a wallflower!'

Hurrying along the rough sandy track, she followed the family into Clockmaker's. Edmund had lit the lamp and Pa was breaking the seal on the bulky letter.

'It's money!' he exclaimed, studying the half-dozen lines scrawled on the thick paper. 'From Rory!'

'It's his writing,' said Edmund, peering over his father's shoulder. 'But it's signed Robbie!'

'Robbie was the pet name your ma and me gave him when he was a bairn – long before any of you came along,' answered Ramsay, adding solemnly. 'Seems he's had need to change his name.'

'Argentina! He's living in Argentina!' read Amy, scarcely able to believe her eyes. 'He's safe and doing well … he must be! That's an awful lot of money!'

'It is that.' Ramsay clumsily bundled it and the letter together, jamming them behind Ma's tea caddy on the dresser. 'And I'll crawl on my hands and knees and beg Alfred Paslew for a job before I'll touch a penny piece of it! Rory's my lad and I'm thankful he's still alive and safe,' he concluded tersely. 'But sure as night follows day, that money's dishonestly come by and Lord alone knows whose and how much blood might be on it!'

Rory's letter was still propped there behind the tea caddy on Boxing Day morning when Amy rose early to make ready for the move to Lane End. She couldn't help but wonder what her brother had done after fleeing Carteret Square, and how he came to prosper so very far away in South America. Placing the letter into Pa's satchel, along with the rest of the family papers and valuables, Amy set to clearing the dressers, cupboards and pantry, and to packing the contents into tea chests.

She, Vicky and Aunt Anne had spent the

days before Christmas scrubbing and scouring at Lane End so that the new house would be clean and ready.

Dan Ainsworth brought the wagon up to Clockmaker's and, after numerous trips back and forth, on foot as well as wheels, by nightfall the MacFarlanes were sitting down to their first meal in their new home.

The bells of All Hallows rang out the old year and rang in the new, and the weeks began slipping by. Everything went on much as before. Vicky went to school, Ramsay persevered with his search for regular work, Edmund studied constantly and became increasingly nervous as his scholarship examination approached, and Amy did all she could to make their new home a comfortable and happy one.

Then, stepping out one evening after she'd been working late at Jessups', she was drawn inexorably down to the deserted shore.

Standing on the damp sand, she breathed deeply, absorbing the power and the wildness; feeling the roar and crash of the tide sweeping up out of the night, billowing and breaking in wavelets just inches from her feet.

Until that moment, she hadn't realised

how she'd pined for the sounds of the sea, which had been constant at Clockmaker's Cottage, regardless of the tide – nor how sorely she'd missed the lonely cry of the gulls and the sharp, fresh salty air.

Turning from the water's edge, her gaze drifted along the strand towards her old home. Standing alone in the darkness, looking at the pale moonshine reflecting upon its blank windows, it disturbed Amy to see the cottage left so desolate and forlorn.

It was for sale now, and she pondered who might buy her old home and what sort of family would make it their own. Then she left the shore and, quickening her pace, began the long walk back into Monks Quay.

Despite the lateness of the hour, a light was showing in the schoolhouse, and Amy knocked at Aunt Anne's door.

'I saw you were still up, so I've brought you this.' She held out a book of poetry. 'Mr Jessup bought a chest of second-hand books from Lancaster and I've been sorting them for the shelves. This is for you.'

'William Cowper! How wonderful!' exclaimed Anne, opening the pages. 'What a handsome volume!'

'I mentioned how much you admired Cowper, and Mr Jessup said you were most welcome to have it!'

'Wasn't that kind of him! And you too, my dear.' Anne smiled, considering her niece. 'I'm pleased the move to Lane End has turned out well for you all. For me, too. It's lovely having you nearby.'

Impulsively, Amy hugged her aunt's bony shoulders. She was keenly aware how attached Anne was to Clockmaker's Cottage, and how deeply saddened she must be by its loss.

'I'm so sorry, Aunt...'

'There, now. It's all right.' She held Amy at arm's length. 'You're looking tired and far too thin. Continue like this, and Gilbert won't recognise you when he returns!'

Amy was resigned. 'There's nothing for him in Monks Quay, Aunt. He said so. Gilbert won't come back.'

'Won't he?' Anne tilted her head. 'If and when he does return, don't waste any time in building your bridges!'

Everyone was abed when Amy let herself into Lane End. Aunt Anne had been right about one thing – she was tired.

Without bothering to heat up her share of the cobbler she'd made for the family's supper, she washed her hands, took the lamp to the table and picked up her sewing.

There wasn't much of this week's batch left to do.

She'd press the work in the morning and take the basket over to Whiteladies before going on to Jessups'.

Mrs Paslew was a generous employer and Amy's wages from the weekly basket of needlework, together with making the curtains for the main downstairs rooms at Whiteladies, were essential to the family. Although Pa did odd jobs around the town, they were struggling without a man's regular wage and, but for Amy's contribution, wouldn't be able to make ends meet.

Sleet was driving down from the distant hills and cutting across the stubbly fields when Amy scurried away from Lane End next morning, taking a short cut through Friars Wood to Whiteladies Grange.

Her head was bowed against the weather and both her arms were wrapped about the sewing basket as she ran the last few yards across the cobbles of the turning circle towards the rear door, realising too late that Alfred Paslew had been watching her approach from the coach-house and was stepping out to block her progress.

'Miss MacFarlane.' His voice was quiet

but brusque. 'I owe you an apology. Over-due, I'm afraid. I acted in haste. Unwisely so, I now believe. That's all. You may continue about your business. Good morning to you.'

He marched back into the coach-house and, astonished, Amy sped the remaining yards across the cobbles to the kitchen.

She was still mulling over this unexpected encounter as she made her way from White-ladies towards Jessups', when Ned Yarkin and her father passed in a great hurry.

'We can't stop!' called Ramsay breath-lessly. 'Ned's just come and tipped me the word that a fellow at the boatyard has taken ill. If I get along there quick, I may get his job!'

'If it's the consumption, he'll not be need-ing it awhile. Maybe not ever,' said Ned Yarkin grimly. 'And it sounded like the consumption to me!'

'Keep your fingers crossed, lass – this'd be right up my street!'

Choir practice wasn't the same without Gil-bert leading it. Nonetheless, Amy attended regularly, and when she arrived home after that evening's session and there was no sign of Pa, she hoped it was because he'd been taken on at the boatyard.

Sure enough, when he came in just as the meal was on the table, Ramsay didn't need to say a word – it was written plain across his face.

'I can turn my hand to most things when it comes to boats – I've had to, over the years,' he declared, handing Amy a flask of local oak cider. 'Mull that for us, lass, and fetch in your Aunt Anne to join us. We'll have a cup – even you, Vicky, with plenty of water – to celebrate me having a proper job again!'

As Amy mixed honey and cloves into the oak cider, added a cinnamon stick and gently warmed the golden concoction, the family's talk around the table was the liveliest she'd heard in many a month.

It was such a blessing to see Pa his old self again. A great burden had been removed from his shoulders.

But although she didn't give them voice, her thoughts strayed to the man who had been taken so poorly, and to those who depended upon him.

'By, that smells grand!' Ramsay beamed at her when she brought the mulled cider to the table. 'I want us to raise our cups, not only to celebrate my new job but to toast

Edmund, who has his examination coming up! Here's to you, my boy!' Ramsay reached across to slap his son's shoulder. 'You're going to do us all proud!'

When the day came for Edmund to go up to Preston to sit his scholarship examination, Amy was struck by how young he looked. She slipped her arm through his as they waited at The Mermaid for the coach.

'Are you sure you'll have enough to read on the journey?' she asked, trying to make him laugh and nodding to the huge bag of books at his feet.

It worked – almost. The flicker of a nervous smile twitched at the corners of his mouth.

'There *are* a lot, aren't there! I'm afraid I'll forget something and need to look it up again before I go into the examination room,' he said.

'I'm sure you won't need them,' reassured Amy. 'But it's sensible to have them with you, just in case.'

Edmund nodded vigorously. 'That's what Gilbert said. I'm glad he's coming up from Oxford to meet me. We're going to revise all this evening and first thing tomorrow, before the examination begins.'

Amy bit back questions she would've liked to ask about Gilbert. She tried not to speak of him too often but it didn't help.

'Don't worry, Edmund. You know your subjects and you'll pass.'

'I have to, Amy. I just have to!' His smooth face creased into an anxious frown. 'Pa has all his hopes pinned on me. I couldn't bear to let him down!'

The coach duly departed and she cheerily waved until it was out of sight, scarcely aware that Dan had come to stand at her side.

'He'll do fine. He's got a grand future ahead of him.'

'He deserves it. I've never known anyone work so hard.'

'Happen he gets that from his big sister!' said Dan, grinning. He shook a newspaper from his coat pocket. *'The Clarion's* just come with the coach. The story about the shares swindle has broken.'

Amy took the paper, folded open at a long article, and immediately saw Dan's name in bold print next to that of the editor.

'My goodness, Dan! Congratulations!'

'I didn't write all of it, I just contributed,' he said, pleased with her enthusiastic reaction. 'Paslew wouldn't speak to me, but the editor gave me a few leads and I tracked down this man, Spofforth. He had plenty to say! He's got a flax mill down over at Croskirk. At least, he did have. Theodore Buxton fleeced him good and proper. Spofforth lost the lot.'

'The newspaper doesn't mention Theo?'

'No. But only because the editor has to be careful about naming names. It's early days yet.'

'If only Fanny and Nick weren't part of Theo's household! It's wrong they have to face the consequences of his wickedness!'

'They're innocent and have nothing to fear,' Dan said, walking with her to Jessups'. 'Which is more than can be said for Theodore Buxton – his worst nightmare is about to come true!'

When Edmund got back to Monks Quay later that week, he stretched out in the comfortable fireside chair and folded his arms across his chest.

'I can't believe it's over. All those books. All those months and months of reading and studying. Of course, if I pass and am offered a place at the school, then the real studying will be just beginning.'

'That's true,' said Amy with a smile, taking

out her crochet.

She was working the sleeve of a jacket to match the bonnet and shawl she'd already made for Fanny's baby.

'Ever since I saw that piece in *The Clarion*, I haven't stopped thinking about Fanny. It can't be very long before her time.'

'Will Theo go to jail?'

'I don't know what'll happen. Although Dan explained it to me as best he could, I still don't quite understand how Theo cheated all those people out of their money.'

'Gilbert said an odd thing,' mused Edmund, after they'd fallen silent for a while. 'He always does ask about you in his letters, but when I saw him in Preston, he asked me if you and Dan were married! He and his father are reconciled, by the way. Gilbert said Mr Paslew has finally accepted there are worse things than having a son who's a clergyman – although probably not many!'

Amy tensed. The notion of Gilbert believing she was married to Dan Ainsworth was peculiarly disconcerting, and the uneasiness stayed with her long after Edmund had mentioned it.

Next morning, as Ramsay got ready for work, Amy was in the kitchen, cutting bread and cheese for him and only half-listening as he expounded upon some tricky aspect of corking.

'...so we got that sorted out and I was just knocking off when Seth Pickering – he has the ships' chandlers at the boatyard, I've known him years – comes across and says he has to go out for a couple of hours, and will I look after the shop for him? So I did, and thoroughly enjoyed it! It's a tidy little business Seth's got there. When he got back, he said that if it suited me he would put a few hours' work my way whenever he needed to go out. It saves shutting the shop. He's on his own, y'see. He was telling me he's had a few assistants in the past, but they always ended up with their fingers in the till so he manages without 'em now.'

Taking his bread and cheese and wrapping his muffler about his neck, Ramsay started out of the kitchen door.

'Oh, something else Seth was telling me – Clockmaker's Cottage is sold. He doesn't know who to. Nobody local, anyhow.'

Amy's spirits sank. That the cottage would one day be sold had been inevitable. However, its occurring now only deepened a despair that refused to lift as the day wore on.

It was mid-afternoon, and she was in Jessups', wrapping a bottle of Indian ink, when Edmund burst into the stationer's.

'Amy – you'd better come!'

Brother and sister sped along Abbotsgate, with Edmund hurriedly explaining he'd been working in the stables as usual when the coach had arrived...

'In here!' He held open the front door of The Mermaid Inn and Amy hurried inside to see Fanny sitting straight-backed before the parlour fire, a pot of tea on the table beside her and her bags, boxes, and the Shawcross walnut corner clock stacked on the floor around her.

'Theo has deserted me, Amy,' she declared, raising furious eyes to her sister. 'I've come home!'

Fanny's daughter was born on the day that the first wild daffodils flowered in Friars Wood. Amy crept upstairs into the room where baby Grace was sleeping contentedly in her mother's arms, and sat beside Fanny's bed.

'She's beautiful, Fan! If only Ma were here to see you both!'

'I've been thinking about Ma, too,' said Fanny. 'She would have loved being a grandma! For his part, Pa is taking his new responsibilities very seriously – I understand it's drinks all round at The Mermaid!'

Amy laughed. 'He's thrilled to bits!'

'Do you think Pa is serious about the ships' chandlers, Amy? For weeks now, it's been a real bee in his bonnet.'

Fanny was right. Pa was much taken with the prospect of buying into the thriving little shop.

'I think he will go into partnership with Seth Pickering one day. It would make good sense for both of them,' considered Amy. 'However, he can't afford it until he sells the Jenet Rae and he's determined to fix her up first, so he can get a good price.'

'It seems everything comes down to profit, doesn't it?' reflected Fanny, smoothing a flaxen curl from Grace's forehead. 'Recently, I've questioned whether Theo ever loved me at all.'

'He adored you, Fanny – I heard him telling Nick so,' replied Amy at once. 'There isn't any doubt Theo loved you!'

'Isn't there?' she queried evenly. 'I knew he'd inherited the house at Carteret Square from his maternal grandfather. However, just before he ran away to avoid being arrested as a common criminal, I discovered

Carteret Square was left to Theo in trust! It became his only upon his marriage.'

'Oh, Fan!' cried Amy. 'You can't think–'

'I can, Amy. And I do,' she replied briskly. 'Theo left me in the final weeks of my confinement, without any thought to me or his unborn child. Heaven knows what I would've done if Nicholas hadn't stayed behind in York to manage the shambles Theo left behind.'

'Nick's a good man,' Amy said quietly. 'He cares deeply for you and Grace.'

'I know he does, and I care deeply for him.' She tenderly kissed Grace's downy cheek. 'I've had ample time and reason to repent marrying the wrong brother.'

On the day Edmund received the results of his scholarship examination, the coach from York brought Nicholas Buxton to Monks Quay.

Deciding to leave Fanny and Nick to talk privately, Amy and Edmund took Vicky and Grace out into the warm sunshine of the spring afternoon.

Edmund's curiosity about Theo's criminal activities was as nothing compared to his euphoria at gaining his scholarship. He'd read the letter at least eight times to Amy's certain knowledge.

'We've a lot to do to get you ready to go, Edmund,' she said practically. 'Easter isn't so far off, and the term starts straight after.'

'I'm really excited.' He beamed. 'But I'm nervous, too! By the time they were my age, Gilbert and Nicholas had already been away at school for years and years. I'm not really looking forward to living in lodgings with total strangers, either.'

'I'm sure the school wouldn't recommend this establishment if it were not clean and respectable,' replied Amy, consulting the letter again. 'Oh, Edmund – a pass with distinction! We're all so very proud of you!'

Late into that night, Amy and Fanny sat up sipping hot cocoa, talking quietly and sharing confidences just as they had done so many times before, when they'd shared the long room under the eaves at Clockmaker's Cottage.

Fanny's fair ringlets gleamed in the soft light as she cradled Grace in her arms and despite all her recent troubles, Amy had never seen her elder sister more composed.

'Nicholas brought me a letter and money from Theo. He is in India,' she explained simply. 'Apparently, when he left me in York, Theo only narrowly avoided arrest. Investors lost a fortune and my husband made one. He's a wealthy man again now, and wants Grace and I to sail with Nicholas to India. He wishes us all to make a fresh start.'

'In India?' echoed Amy in consternation. 'When is Nick sailing?'

'The week after next.'

'At least it gives you a little time to make up your mind.'

'I don't need any time,' said Fanny, drawing the soft wool of the crocheted shawl closer about her daughter. 'I'd already reached a decision concerning my marriage long before Nicholas brought Theo's letter. Grace and I are settled here in Monks Quay. I'm not inclined to leave again.'

'If that's what you truly want – then I'm so glad, Fan!'

'Well, honestly, imagine what the blazing sun would do to my complexion!' she returned. 'And I'd be constantly worried lest my hair started to look horsey.'

Amy laughed out loud. 'You don't change, Fanny!'

'I do, Amy. And I have,' she murmured seriously. 'For the better, I think.'

'What of Nick? Will he stay out in India?'

'Nicholas loves his brother, Amy. Nothing

will ever change that. He wants to do the honourable thing and see Theo face to face. That's very important to him. But no, he won't stay in India.' Fanny met Amy's gaze steadily. 'Nicholas also wishes to make his home and future here in Monks Quay.'

Nicholas Buxton accompanied the Mac-Farlanes to All Hallows on the following Sunday morning, pausing to shake hands and pay his respects to the Paslews as he passed by their family pew.

Fanny had been worried that Grace might start to cry, but from her seat at the front of the choir stalls, Amy could see that her little niece was perfectly content and didn't even bat an eyelid when the organ groaned into life and Aunt Anne struck the opening chords of the first hymn.

When the singing began, an achingly familiar tenor voice unexpectedly flooded Amy's senses. She couldn't glance around as the service unfolded, but she was increasingly aware of Gilbert's presence just a yard or so behind her.

She heard not a word of Reverend Linley's sermon until he actually mentioned Gilbert by name and then her attention riveted upon the elderly man.

'Gilbert Paslew has been ordained in holy orders, and Monks Quay is to be his first curacy. I feel doubly blessed,' went on William Linley, 'because not only at long last do I have a curate to assist me, but the said curate is my own dear nephew. We are both eagerly anticipating working together and serving our parishioners. Indeed, next week, Gilbert will be conducting the christening of little Grace, who is with us this morning and, unlike some other members of the congregation, is still awake. Now, for our final hymn...'

As was the custom, the choir remained seated while the congregation filed out, but when All Hallows was almost empty and the choir were rising to leave, Amy was aware of Gilbert moving to her side and her intention of slipping away without seeing him was dashed.

'Amy?'

Awkwardly, she half-turned but did not raise her eyes, fumbling instead with her music.

'Amy,' he went on softly. 'May I walk with you?'

An excuse – any excuse – was on the tip of her tongue. She didn't want to walk with him or be with him or speak to him. It would open old wounds and hurt too much. Already, the longing for him that she'd begun to hope had grown dull, was slicing through her as keenly as upon the night they'd parted.

But everyone else had gone, and she and Gilbert were alone. The quietness drummed unbearably inside her ears. The dancing shafts of brilliant sunlight and the potent fragrance of spring flowers were making her dizzy and the whitewashed walls and stone floor of the ancient church swam before her eyes. She desperately wanted to escape this closeness and be out in the cool, reviving fresh air and to have these awful moments over and done with But it could not be avoided. Gilbert was curate at All Hallows now and she'd have to become accustomed to being in his presence.

Taking a deep breath, she inclined her head and moved from the choir stalls, walking slightly ahead of him from the church. Once outside, he fell into step beside her and they set off across the meadows, down towards the sea, just as they'd done upon so many other Sundays.

'I'd imagined you would be married to Dan Ainsworth,' he began hesitantly. 'Then I found it wasn't so. Not yet, at least. Do you and he have intentions, Amy?'

'No, we do not!' she retorted, her eyes fixed upon the horizon as they walked. 'Dan and I are old friends, that is all!'

'Oh, are you, indeed?' he questioned quietly. 'The night I came to Clockmaker's Cottage to tell you I was going to Oxford and to ask you to wait for me, Dan Ainsworth was there with you! I heard the way he spoke to you, Amy. Saw the way he looked at you. When I reached for you, you shrank away,' he concluded harshly. 'What was I supposed to think? You couldn't bear to let me touch you!'

Shaking her head in disbelief, Amy rounded on him, her eyes blazing. 'If only you knew–'

Gilbert caught his breath, gazing down at her, searching the depths of her eyes. And suddenly, he *did* know.

'Amy–' he spoke her name urgently, pulling her to him. 'I love you and I never want to lose you again! I want you to be mine!'

'I've always been yours,' she whispered brokenly as he took her in his arms.

'There's something I should tell you,' he began simply, as they continued their stroll along the shore. 'When I heard that Clockmaker's Cottage was for sale, I bought it ... in the hope you'd consider becoming my wife and would consent to live there with me.'

They had reached the cottage gate, and his arm encircled her slender waist.

'Will you?' He smiled between kisses. 'Has that Dog Star of yours led me on a true course?'

Breathlessly, Amy laughed. 'Gilbert ... the Dog Star has brought us both safely home.'

The publishers hope that this book has given you enjoyable reading. Large Print Books are especially designed to be as easy to see and hold as possible. If you wish a complete list of our books please ask at your local library or write directly to:

Dales Large Print Books
Magna House, Long Preston,
Skipton, North Yorkshire.
BD23 4ND

This Large Print Book, for people
who cannot read normal print,
is published under the auspices of

THE ULVERSCROFT FOUNDATION

... we hope you have enjoyed this book.
Please think for a moment about those
who have worse eyesight than you ...
and are unable to even read or enjoy
Large Print without great difficulty.

You can help them by sending a
donation, large or small, to:

**The Ulverscroft Foundation,
1, The Green, Bradgate Road,
Anstey, Leicestershire, LE7 7FU,
England.**
or request a copy of our brochure for
more details.

The Foundation will use all donations
to assist those people who are visually
impaired and need special attention
with medical research, diagnosis
and treatment.

Thank you very much for your help.